I0733813

THE CORPSE IN THE COURTYARD

A JACOB AND MIRIAM MYSTERY

BOOK 3

RICHARD FREEBORN

CONTENTS

COPYRIGHT

The Corpse in the Courtyard

Copyright © 2024 by Richard Freeborn

Cover and layout: Copyright © 2024 by Richard Freeborn

Cover Art Copyright © swisshippo (Fedor Selivanov)

Author Photograph Copyright © 2024 by Jacqueline Olivie

ISBN-13: 978-1-958214-07-7

This book is licensed for your personal enjoyment only. All rights reserved. This is a work of fiction. All characters and events portrayed in this book are fictional, and any resemblance to real people or incidents is purely coincidental. This book, or parts thereof, may not be reproduced in any form without permission.

NO AI TRAINING: Without in any way limiting the author's exclusive rights under copyright, any use of this publication to "train" generative artificial intelligence (AI) technologies to generate text is expressly prohibited. The author reserves all rights to license uses of this work for generative AI training and development of machine learning language models.

 Created with Vellum

In memory of Chris Petford

It is said friends come to you for a reason, a season, or for life

She is a lifer

PROLOG

The fifteenth day of Simanu - Afternoon

The army camp at Borsippa a half-day ride west of the city of Babylon was a sprawling mass of tents, storehouses, stables, and men marching, training, and hurrying from one place to another.

A cloud of dust hung in the air, stirred by the constant activity of hundreds of soldiers. A thin coating of beige dust covered cloaks and tents and everything left uncovered.

Ligish, Commander of the Guard at the Esagila, the temple complex that oversaw the religious life of Babylon, kept a cloth over his face to protect his nose and mouth. He walked his horse along the tent line, careful to avoid the web of ropes and stakes that kept the tents from collapsing.

At the end of the tent line, a pair of sentries watched Ligish approach. They checked on him but kept their attention on either side, not allowing his approach to distract them from any other potential danger.

Ligish nodded in approval. These men knew their job.

There were rumors in Babylon - in the Esagila, and even the Court of King Nebuchadnezzar - that the long campaign in Lebanon had drained the military. The army was not what it once had been; the rumors said.

Any new conflict would find them wanting.

In his opinion, the rumors were the gossip of idle tongues. The rumors had said the same before the siege of Jerusalem and the subjugation of the Judeans. Ligish suspected it had been the same forty or more years before when Babylon and Elam joined forces to defeat the Assyrians and sack Nineveh.

The clash of spears being brought down across his path pulled Ligish from his thoughts.

"What is your business with the general?" The older of the two guards demanded. He looked barely twenty summers, but Ligish knew the dark, empty look in the man's eyes.

Too many battles. Too many deaths.

Ligish hoped the guards saw something different in his own eyes, but suspected they saw that same dark, empty look.

He pulled a round, gold token from a pocket in his tunic, leaned down and offered it to the guard. "I am Ligish of the Esagila. I am sent by Priest Arioch to ask a favor of your general."

The guard shifted the spear upright so he could control it better, then leaned forward to study the token more closely. Whatever he saw in the symbols satisfied him. He gave a hand signal to his companion. The two soldiers lifted their spears and stood aside.

"You must walk from here. The officer at the third tent will take you further."

Ligish replaced the token in his tunic, dismounted.

General Nebuzaraddan's tent was really two large tents joined together. One for sleeping in, the other for administrative work. A wide awning covered the front of both tents. Under the awning were two couches with straw-filled cushions, and an iron brazier, cold now in the heat of summer, but essential if a campaign ran into fall and winter.

The layout was familiar to Ligish. He remembered it from the Judah campaign, and the first thrusts into Lebanon once the deportations from Jerusalem began.

"Ligish. I'd like to think you're here to beg me for a return to real soldiering, but your fancy uniform makes me believe otherwise."

Ligish turned at the voice behind him. Nebuzaraddan looked much the same as he had when Ligish served under him. Iron-gray hair trimmed close to his head, his spade-shaped beard trimmed shorter than the current fashion, and gray eyes that assessed under the sparkle of pleasure at seeing Ligish.

"There are times I would welcome a simple charge into the swords and spears of a known enemy." Ligish said. He returned the General's hug of welcome.

"I warned you," Nebuzaraddan said as an orderly ducked his head and came under the awning with a tray of fruit and a jug of wine.

Nebuzaraddan waved toward the couches. "I have time to reminisce with an old comrade. First, tell me what Arioch wants."

It didn't surprise Ligish that Nebuzaradan suspected a purpose behind the visit.

"We have a situation at the Esagila," Ligish said, accepting a goblet of wine.

"At the last New Year Festival, silver was stolen from inside the Esagila. We found the thieves, but not those behind the thieves. More recently, two shipments of grain for the Eanna temple in Erech were spoiled, and we found vermin in the storerooms."

"Aimed at Arioch or the Esagila?"

Ligish shrugged. "I don't know. My belief is these are attacks with a goal to remove Arioch. I think it's someone inside the Esagila, but I can't prove it, and I can't trust anyone."

Nebuzaraddan frowned over the rim of his own wine goblet.

"And I can help you how?"

"You have one of the Judean Exiles training skirmishers and groups that disrupt an enemy. One of his countrymen gave me his name. They served together in the Judean army. I want to borrow Asher to find these people for me."

Nebuzaraddan frowned again, took a sip of his wine, and nodded to himself. Ligish could never interpret the look on Nezaruddan's face. He felt his stomach twist, partly in anticipation and partly in fear Nezaruddan would deny the request.

The general nodded again. "Very well, but with two conditions, Ligish. Asher must agree to this, and I want him back within four moons. The King is considering another invasion of Egypt, and I will need Asher's skills for that." He reached for the wine jug and refilled their goblets. "Now tell me what's happening with your family."

CHAPTER ONE

Two months later
The fourth day of Abu - Before Dawn

Jacob woke the way he always did. Waking was a transition from sleep to awareness without the fuzzy twilight time many people experienced. The fuzziness only happened when he was wounded or injured.

Jacob lay on the straw mattress. He felt unsettled, but couldn't work out why. After a moment, he pushed the thoughts away and rolled over to his right side. The straw mattress rustled under him, some sharp ends poking at his ribs. Jacob ignored them and pushed the thin wool blanket off his chest and stomach, trying to get some air across his body.

It was mid-summer here in Babylon, and an oppressive heat had settled over the city three days before. Night time offered no relief and on each successive day the heat felt worse.

The heat made it impossible to work outside for most of the day. Jacob had attempted it and nearly fallen from the roof of the house he was building. He shook his head and smiled at the memory.

Not his best moment.

Thankfully, he had reached out and hooked his left arm round a piece of wood to avoid a serious fall.

Even now, two days later, Jacob shivered at the thought of trying to save himself by using just his weakened right arm. The muscles in his arm had never recovered from the wound inflicted by a Babylonian soldier during the siege of Jerusalem. The arm would never have held his weight.

The house he was building stood alone between the Inner Walls and the Outer Ramparts of Babylon, shielded from its neighbors by fruit orchards. If Jacob had fallen, it was unlikely anyone would hear his cries.

Not like Jerusalem, where inside or outside the city walls, it seemed everyone knew everyone's business.

Jacob shifted his body again as nostalgia twisted his stomach. It was five long years since the Judeans had been forced into Exile by their Babylonian conquerors. He missed Jerusalem, the city of his birth, as much now as he had in those first months. Located high above the Judean plains, Jerusalem in mid-summer was a much cooler and much more pleasant place to live.

Jacob had built the house with the courtyard facing north, so it received the benefit of the prevailing wind for most of the year. Of course, at this time of year, when the weather was hottest, the prevailing wind shifted to come from the west. He smiled at that thought and considered the progress made over the past month.

When the house was complete, this room where he lay would be for guests. The open doorway giving access to the expansive courtyard that looked over orchards and small fields of corn and barley. Three other bedrooms completed this side of the house. One was for himself and Miriam, the woman he expected to marry within the next two moons. The others for the children he hoped for, although he had barely discussed the possibility with Miriam.

They were at least ten years older than other couples beginning a marriage, so perhaps there would be no children in their future. If that was the case, the rooms would be for guests.

Jacob shifted and rolled over again, seeing the slight fading of the night through the open doorway, and a thin rind of light creeping up from the eastern horizon.

Jacob estimated it was maybe an hour before sunrise, possibly a little longer. The time worried Jacob. He usually woke closer to the dawn, leaving himself enough time to dress and greet the rising sun with the morning Shema prayer.

It was too early for the birds to be moving in the orchards, and no noise from the rooster in the closest house over a hundred paces away.

The unsettled feeling returned, and now Jacob knew why.

Something, or someone, had disturbed him.

Jacob rolled off the mattress, slipped into a loose tunic and trews, pulled a short sword from the scabbard underneath his mattress, hefted the sword in his left hand, accustoming his arm once again to the weight and balance of the weapon.

Before the Exile, he had been a soldier. The habits he had learned a dozen years ago as a teenager remained with him.

Jacob crouched low, eased out of the room into the courtyard.

He moved slowly, a hand-span at a time, in case someone watched the house. The westerly wind, barely a breeze, eddied over the roof and moved the hot air from one place to another, providing no relief, bringing with it the heat smell like an empty pot left over a fire for too long.

He saw no movement, heard nothing except the chatter of the insects now he was out in the open. The insect hum told Jacob whoever, or whatever, had been here was gone. He relaxed a small amount, but kept the sword at the ready as he let his gaze travel over the outline of the building.

To his right, the house was almost finished. There was still work needed to cover the mud-brick walls, and Jacob wanted to add proper wooden doors rather than the cured hide panels the Babylonians favored.

On the left, with walls barely above waist height, were the servant's quarters, and two rooms he considered the most important. The nearest room was Miriam's workroom, where she could dry herbs and prepare the salves and tonics that many of the Exiles, especially the women, asked her to prepare.

Next to Miriam's workroom was the kitchen. Jacob didn't want a kitchen capable of preparing enormous feasts. He wanted a kitchen large enough to cook for ten or twenty people so he could repay the hospitality many Exiles and Babylonians had shown him over the five years of Exile.

There were piles of mud-bricks and lengths of Lebanese cedar stacked beside the walls. Everything angular and sharp-edged, as it should be.

A part of Jacob wanted to relax, to walk across the courtyard and relax on one of the wooden couches and meditate until the sun lifted over the horizon and he could celebrate the Shema prayer. He turned, studied the opposite side of the courtyard where the rooms were finished, and at the end of the eastern side of the wall, he saw a heap of something out of place.

The heap could be debris and waste waiting to be cleared away.

Jacob didn't think so. He had placed nothing on that side of the house in the last six or seven days.

He stayed beside the wall, feeling the rough brick scrape across his right shoulder.

His heart pounded hard in his chest. Jacob felt the lift of awareness that always came just before a skirmish or battle. Any feeling or thought of tiredness or fatigue disappeared.

Jacob kept his right side close to the wall, glanced behind him. It was a habit he learned while leading his soldiers on night raids against the Babylonian army during the siege of Jerusalem.

There was no-one behind him. He hadn't expected there to be. Only two of those soldiers remained alive.

The memory made him shiver. He pushed the thought aside, crept slowly along the wall toward the pile.

Fifteen paces away, he felt the slick twist in his gut as he recognized the pile for what it was.

Jacob lowered the sword and changed direction toward the half-finished kitchen. He placed the sword on the top of the waist-high wall, picked up a sliver of kindling, and uncovered the embers of the cooking fire. He blew carefully on the ashes until they glowed bright red in the semi-darkness, then pushed the kindling in, holding it there until light flared.

Shielding the flame with his right hand, Jacob touched the kindling to the wick of a sesame oil lamp placed beside the fireplace. He held the burning kindling against the wick until the flame was all burning sesame oil.

The line of light on the eastern horizon was wider and brighter, but Jacob still needed the lamp to see properly as he reached the pile.

What at first appeared to be rags was a ripped cloak bundled round a body. The legs were bound with rags, the left foot twisted at an impossible angle.

Jacob reached with his left hand for the shoulder of the cloak and rolled the body over. As the body shifted, the cloak flapped open, revealing a naked torso with bruises and wounds across the stomach, chest, and neck.

The man's face was a bloodied mask, his nose broken, eyes wide and looking at the sky without seeing.

Jacob felt the chill run up his spine. His throat closed up and tears sprang into his eyes. Jacob reached over and gently closed the man's eyes, saying a prayer as he did so.

Palti. Nabu. Eleazar. Ithamara.

And now Asher.

Five soldiers who fought for Jerusalem and Judah.

Jacob was now the only one alive.

CHAPTER TWO

The fourth day of Abu - Early Morning

The prayer shawl was heavy and scratchy on Miriam's shoulders. She tried lifting the shawl, moving it so she could get air to her neck and shoulders. The challenge was the air was hot and dry. Even the slight movement of the shawl was no relief. It made the heat feel worse.

She had slept poorly. A combination of her courses, and the hot air, heavy and oppressive over Babylon's Inner City. The closely packed mud-brick buildings absorbed the burning heat of the day and let it out at night, making every room seem close to a furnace like the ones burning day and night in the village of Kweiresh to the north of the city.

Miriam stood in the courtyard of the house belonging to her cousin, Esther's family. The family had taken her in during the trek into Exile after Miriam's husband disappeared. The search found nothing. Her husband was presumed dead, leaving Miriam a widow.

Esther stood next to Miriam, shorter by a head, thick around the waist, and heavy in the breast. She was six years older than Miriam and beads of perspiration sparkled on her brow as she tried to keep her two young sons attentive while her husband Isaac led the recital of the morning Shema prayer.

As the daughter, and widow, of priests, Miriam knew the words and cadence of Shema well enough that she could make the responses automatically.

Today, though, despite the heat and her cramping abdomen, she felt the prayers were important, more deserving of her attention than usual. She didn't like this feeling.

Usually, when this happened, it meant something was wrong somewhere in her life.

As Isaac finished the last prayer, Miriam offered a prayer of her own, asking that Jacob be safe. She could deal with troubles of her own, but feared for Jacob.

With her personal devotion completed, Miriam slipped the shawl off her shoulders and folded it. The wool felt damp where it had laid across her back. Many more days of this heat and the shawl would require washing, or it would smell bad and distract everyone from Shema.

As she draped the shawl over her arm, Esther's youngest darted away from his mother toward the doorway into the street, where Isaac talked with a man Miriam didn't recognize.

Miriam bent down, hooked her arm round the boy's waist, let his momentum swing him off his feet. He hung on her arm, legs flailing, voice wailing until Esther relieved Miriam of the burden.

"We eat first, then you have lessons," Esther said to her son. She hoisted him in her arms and carried him across to the table where the servants were laying out plates of fruit and nuts, and jugs of water.

Miriam waited for the boys to settle before taking her place on the long bench that let her see the full expanse of the courtyard. To her left, stairs led up to a balcony and the second story. Opposite the stairs were the doors to the kitchen. Miriam gave thanks she had no responsibilities there, for even with the cooking fire banked down to embers, it would be burning hot inside.

She reached for a handful of dates, then let them fall as she caught one of the water jugs, toppled by the eldest boy, and set it upright and out of his reach.

"I don't know if it's the heat, or a joint attempt by the boys to put me out of my mind," Esther said as she joined Miriam on the bench. She tilted her head and studied Miriam. "Are you all right?"

Miriam nodded, picked up a handful of dates without incident. "The heat, I expect," and then in a lower voice so only Esther could hear. "And the last of my courses."

"Then stay out of the sun and drink water," Esther said.

"I'll do that."

Miriam had a selection of dried herbs ready to be crushed and blended. The work would keep her occupied.

Water was a good idea as well. Miriam poured herself a goblet full, then a second, which she handed to Isaac as he dropped onto the bench opposite.

A big man with wide shoulders and a belly rounding to fat, Isaac's weight made the bench creak, and the table shudder. His round chubby face was already flushed with the heat. He downed the water in one long swallow, poured another, and reached for the melon slices. The flush had faded, but bright scarlet spots persisted high on his cheeks.

Whatever message the stranger had brought, Miriam guessed it had upset and angered Isaac.

Miriam considered asking Isaac about it, but he spoke first.

"Miriam, do you know where Jacob is today?"

"Not for certain. He worked at the house yesterday and planned to sleep there overnight. I expect that's the best place to look for him. Is something wrong?"

"Probably," Isaac said, reaching out and capturing his oldest son's hand in his own as the boy made to throw a date at his brother. "Any more of that and there'll be extra lessons for both of you."

Isaac returned his attention to Miriam, something different in his voice. "The man was a messenger from the caravan grounds. My men were leaving for Erech at first light when guards from the temple of Marduk stopped them. It seems the travel permits issued by the temple have been revoked."

"Just yours, or every merchant?" Esther didn't sound worried.

"Every Judean merchant, and every merchant associated with Judeans. Bel Ibni had two caravans stopped," Isaac said.

This time Miriam recognized the something different. Isaac was anxious. Jacob would be just as concerned. He was Bel Ibni's business manager.

"If Jacob has heard about it, I'm sure he's on his way to the temple of Marduk," Miriam said.

"The temple is my next destination," Jacob said from the street doorway where he stood beside Solly, the elderly retainer who had been with Isaac's family for many years. Now, Solly performed the duties of door guard, and occasional chaperone for Miriam.

Miriam thought Jacob sounded exhausted.

She looked closely at him, saw the pain on his face. It was something bone-deep and searing. His shoulders slumped and his face looked haggard. His tunic was scuffed and stained with what looked like blood.

She grabbed her water goblet, wriggled out of the seat, and took it to him. "Drink this. What happened? Are you hurt?"

He swayed a little, and she had her arm under his left shoulder, holding him up, guiding him to the table. One part of her registered surprise he didn't protest and pull away. Another part enjoyed the feel of his lean, muscular body under her hands.

"Esther, take the boys inside and bring us wine," Isaac said as Miriam eased Jacob into the empty chair at the end of the table.

Miriam sat on the bench, still holding Jacob's hand. The smears on the sleeve really were blood, and she felt her heart skip a bit and her stomach twist. "There's blood on you. Where are you hurt?"

He squeezed her fingers and gave her a weak smile. "I'm not hurt," he said. "At least, not in the way you're thinking. Give me a minute, and thank you, Isaac. I know it's early, but wine would be most welcome."

The wine was brought out, blessed, and poured. Jacob took a sip, then a full mouthful. He released a long sigh as he placed the wine goblet carefully on the table and twirled it slowly with his fingers. When he spoke, it was like he was talking to the wine and not to Miriam, Esther, or Isaac.

"I slept at the new house last night so I could work a long day and hopefully get the walls of Miriam's work room completed. Something woke me about an hour before sunrise. I found a body left at the edge of the courtyard."

He looked at Miriam then. His brown eyes were bright, and there were tears on his cheeks.

"It was Asher. He'd been beaten and tortured."

Miriam felt the tears flood her own eyes and face. She had met Asher on three occasions and liked him a lot. She felt for Jacob's hand again.

All those years around priests and she still did not know what to say or how to offer comfort at times like this.

It was Isaac who saved her.

"Why leave him on your doorstep?"

Jacob stopped twirling the goblet, lifted it, and took another long swallow. "A warning, perhaps. My association with Asher is well known. I gave his name to Ligish of the temple guard, about two moons ago. There have been several incidents within the temple where the culprits have been caught. Unfortunately, those masterminding the disruption remain unknown."

"The silver at New Year?" Miriam asked.

Jacob nodded. "That and others. Ligish doesn't trust anyone other than Arioch, which is sensible of him. He asked for my help and I suggested Asher."

"And Asher agreed to work with them?" Isaac said, pouring more wine into Jacob's goblet.

Jacob nodded again. "Asher spoke to me after Ligish approached him. I told him to be careful, but he laughed like he always did, and said that was his middle name. They burned a symbol of the Esagila into his left cheek."

"That's why you're going to the temple," Esther said. She had joined them in time to hear the last exchange.

"I am, but it seems there's another reason for my visit. What happened, Isaac?"

Quickly, Isaac retold the story of the permits for the caravans. Jacob scowled at the news. Miriam was pleased to see some life coming back into his face, but wished it could have been achieved some other way.

"There is one more thing," Jacob said. "It's why I came here before going to the Esagila. Asher's body must be washed and prepared for burial. He has no family. I know it's much to ask of you, Miriam, especially as traditionally a man should prepare another man for burial, but would you do this for me? For him?"

She knew what he was asking. It was more than a break with tradition. Jacob was asking her to lead the ceremony, and she wasn't sure she could do it, no matter how many times she had taken part in the past.

Miriam drew breath to ask if there was another way, but Esther spoke first.

"I'll come with you and help. We'll collect Rachel on the way. Her family will have a shroud, they are always prepared for everything. The three of us will watch and be his shomers." She looked at Jacob. "Where will you bury him?"

"I haven't thought that far ahead." Jacob shrugged, looking lost again. "I'll talk to our priests, hopefully Ezra, and ask their advice."

"What about," Miriam said, and waited until the others gave her their full attention. "What about the almond orchard on the slope outside the house? You are his family, Jacob, and after we are married, I will be as well. Let Asher rest there, so he can see the dawn every morning."

Miriam knew from the look on Jacob's face she had said the right thing.

CHAPTER THREE

The guard at the side gate of the Esagila recognized Jacob and let him wait inside the gate while he sent a trainee to find Guard Commander Ligish.

The area inside the walls of the Esagila was the largest open space in the Inner City of Babylon. Supposedly, it was larger even than the open areas in Nebuchadnezzar's palace a thousand paces to the north, and definitely larger than the Summer Palace built north of the Inner City walls. Jacob had no direct experience of either palace, and no wish to change that. He was content to rely on the stories from those who visited the palaces.

He doubted the open spaces around the palaces were as chaotic as the Esagila this morning. To his left, pens of sheep and goats bleated a discordant noise, like hundreds of singers performing different songs. The ripe, pungent smell of their waste hung heavy in the hot, still air.

Competing with the noise of the animals, tens of merchants bartered and negotiated with temple priests for the fruits, vegetables, and cages of birds stacked on benches and carts. Acolytes and servants moved constantly, carrying clay tablets, recording the contracts, or guiding the merchants to places where the goods were unloaded.

Directly opposite where Jacob stood, and built high above the banks of the Euphrates, the temple of Marduk dominated the whole Esagila complex, just as it dominated the religious lives of every Babylonian. The Babylonians were free to worship whatever gods they chose, and it seemed to Jacob there was a temple to some god or deity in almost every corner of the city.

It never made sense to Jacob why the Babylonians, Egyptians, even the Greeks, worshipped so many gods. It seemed they had a constant juggling of offerings to different gods for health, wealth, or just a safe journey from one city to another.

Jacob watched the organized chaos around him. He had discussed the different gods many times with Ezra, one of the few Judean priests he trusted, and they both agreed trying to understand was a futile exercise. The Babylonians would never acknowledge Yahweh as the one true God, and the Exile had shown the Judeans what happened when they abandoned their faith for craven images.

There was a movement in the crowd, and Jacob saw Ligish before the other man saw him. In normal times, Ligish moved smoothly and easily, weaving through a crowd and gone before anyone realized he was there.

This morning, he maintained a straight line from the entrance to the storage rooms, across the courtyard, knocking into people and pushing them aside as he moved. The trainee sent by the gate guard trailed behind.

The manner of his walk made Jacob think Ligish was angry, but as he got closer, Jacob saw the look of distraction. He paused when he reached Jacob, his breath coming in long gulps, the sweat beading his forehead, slicking his dark brown hair close to his skull. His eyes, the same dark brown as his hair, studied Jacob, taking in the rumpled tunic, the bloodstains on the sleeve.

Something shifted in his eyes. His shoulders slumped a little. "Asher?"

Jacob nodded.

Ligish exhaled a long sigh, jerked his head back the way he had come.

"We'll do this with Arioch. It will save telling the story twice."

Once inside the building, Ligish led Jacob along wide corridors, and then into a huge, well-lit hall. Rows of scribes sat at desks, carefully transcribing details of every transaction and delivery. It was the first time Jacob had been to Arioch's office, and the sheer size of it surprised him. On his right, a row of windows let in light and looked east along Marduk Street to the Marduk Gate, and beyond where the orchards and barley fields shimmered in the heat.

Wax covered wooden boards covered the opposite wall, some almost covered with symbols, others almost empty. Above each board, an oblong clay tablet hung on the wall and explained the purpose of that board: sheep, barley, wine, and spices.

Three resting couches with ornate silk cushions took up the front of the room. A long table covered with papyrus scrolls and clay tablets sat at the far end of the room. A silver-colored cat sat on the desk, washing herself slowly and carefully. She paused as Jacob and Ligish entered the room. The cat studied Jacob with bright green eyes, then exhaled a soft meow and jumped down. Tail held high, she disappeared through a doorway behind the table.

Arioch, senior priest of the Esagila, and the man responsible for all temple trading, stood in the doorway. His dark eyes studied Jacob for a moment.

"Bring us wine," he said to someone in the next room, then turned his attention back to Jacob. "From the look of you, and the expression Ligish has, I suspect I will not like what you have to tell me."

"Probably not," Jacob said. He glanced behind him where some scribes had paused their work to watch with interest. "Can we talk here without being overheard?"

"The doors are solid," Ligish said. He moved to pull the doors together, settling them in place with a deep thud.

Jacob watched, relieved the doors were solid wood. Lebanese cedar probably, from the way they shone in the light from the windows. Much better than cured ox-hide, and much harder to hear through.

A servant brought a jug of wine and bowls of dates. He placed the bowls on low tables by the resting couches, poured wine, and retreated, closing the door behind him.

Jacob took a sip of the wine. It was rough, sharp over his tongue, and burned down his throat. Not the best wine Arioch could serve, and certainly not the high quality Nineveh wines Jacob had sold the temple a moon previously.

Arioch was sending him a message.

Jacob wasn't sure what that message was, but suspected he was about to find out. He put the wine goblet down on the low table. He needed to be careful and stay alert, especially after the wine he had drunk earlier with Isaac.

Noise of the ongoing negotiations floated up through the windows from the courtyard below. Ligish broke the silence between them. "What happened, Jacob?"

"Someone left Asher's body outside my house just before dawn this morning."

"You're sure it was Asher?"

Jacob pushed the right sleeve of his tunic to the shoulder, revealing the scar from the sword slash that had nearly killed him.

"Asher was beside me the day this happened. He saved my life."

"And during your trek into Babylon, you repaid that debt," Ligish said. "Asher told me the story late one night. The night he asked me to include you."

"Include me in what?"

"Asher was working for me," Arioch said in the low growl Jacob had learned meant the priest was very frustrated. "You suggested his name to Ligish two or three moons ago. Someone to help us uncover the person or people behind the regular occurrence of supposedly unfortunate incidents at the temple."

"Asher agreed to help us," Ligish said, taking a sip of the wine, his cheeks hollowing as he sucked in a sharp breath.

"We met four days ago at the tavern your man Gideon owns. Asher wanted me to let him approach you. He thought he was close to learning who was behind all of this and needed more help."

Jacob put the wine goblet down, helped himself to a handful of dates. The rich, sweet flavor of the fruit on his tongue took away the bite of the wine. "What did you say?"

"I would have preferred your involvement in this from the beginning," Ligish said. "We agreed he would talk with you."

"This morning is the first time I've seen Asher in three or four moons," Jacob said.

Probably closer to five, Jacob thought as he counted the months back in his head. He had meant to make the time, learn when Asher was free from his duties to the Babylonian army, spend a weekend. Their friendship was one that didn't need constant feeding. Soon after the Exiles arrived in Babylon, Asher had been with their army for nearly a year. When they finally met again, it had taken less than an hour to drop back into the easy and comfortable friendship they had shared for many years.

Jacob dropped his head. He would miss Asher.

"Jacob?"

Jacob sat up. Ligish looked at him with concern.

"Are you all right?"

"I will be. It's been a while since I saw Asher. What did he want me for?"

"We aren't certain," Arioch said. He balanced a trio of dates in his palm, rolling them around like he was deciding which one to choose first.

Or, Jacob thought, deciding exactly how much to tell.

"Let me make it easier for you," Jacob said. He knew Miriam would be upset, also that she would understand. "I will find who tortured and killed Asher, and I will find those responsible for what is happening in your temple."

Arioch looked pleased, ate all three dates together, then brushed crumbs off his robe, and stood. "I have other duties that need my attention."

"There's one more thing," Jacob said. "Why did you cancel the trading permits?"

Arioch sat down, the pleasure on his face turning into a hard frown. "To teach you a lesson, Jacob. To teach all of you Judeans a lesson. You knew the temple of Marduk intended to send a caravan to Nineveh, and you went there first and cheated the temple out of wine for the next two seasons. Your people always push boundaries, Jacob. This time, you pushed too hard. If you don't change your ways, I may exercise the right of the temple to confiscate everything your Judah caravan brings back."

This time, Arioch made it all the way to his feet. "Ligish can tell you everything we know. When you bring me the people behind this, Jacob, I will reinstate the permits."

<hr>

CHAPTER FOUR

<hr>

It was early in the afternoon when Miriam, with Esther and Rachel on each side, arrived at the house Jacob was building outside the Inner City walls.

She estimated six or seven days had passed since she last visited the house. As the three of them walked through the orchard of almond trees and up the slight incline to the building, Miriam was amazed at the changes and the amount of work Jacob had completed in such a short time.

When they reached the courtyard, Miriam placed her bag of oils and cloth on the ground and waited while Esther and Rachel relieved themselves of their own burdens.

Only then did Miriam take the time to look more closely at the progress.

The living area of the house looked almost complete, part of it even had a roof. To her right, the servants' quarters, the kitchen, and her workroom had progressed from lines in the dirt to solid waist-high walls of mud-brick.

Beyond the kitchen, the ground was clear of scrub and vegetation, tilled and turned, ready for herbs and vegetables when the weather grew cooler.

"I think I may hate you again," Esther said. There was no venom in her tone, more envy, and Miriam saw that envy in Esther's brown eyes as her cousin studied the layout of the workroom. "Isaac would never consider a room this size worthwhile."

"I told Jacob everything I wanted to do in my workroom and he made it happen," Miriam said with a blush that wasn't all because of the heat.

"And a well in your kitchen?" Rachel said, looking over the top of the half-built wall. She was a short, slender woman. Her head barely came up to Miriam's shoulder, but she had a seemingly endless store of energy, which she needed with her young son. "Do not show this to Samuel. It could hurt Jacob's friendship with my husband."

Esther laughed at Rachel's words. Miriam couldn't join them in their joy. Her attention was drawn to the doorway beyond the half-finished kitchen and workroom. She made her way to the doorway and stepped inside.

The heat inside was more intense than in the courtyard. The sour smell of rotten meat was heavy in the air. Miriam covered her mouth with her hand. She looked at the body laid out on the straw mattress. Jacob had covered Asher with a thin blanket and only his face was visible.

Miriam had met Asher on three occasions and liked him. The battered, misshapen face before her looked nothing like the man she remembered. Deep inside, she knew she would not like what they found on his body once they removed the sheet.

She sensed a movement behind her, turned, and saw Esther with her hand over her mouth. Esther used her other hand to wave Miriam out of the room, back into the open air.

"We cannot work on him in there," Esther said, waving her hand across her face like it would dispel the smell that still seemed to cling to both of them. "At best, only one of us will pass out."

Miriam agreed. A few moments in the room were more than enough for her head and stomach. She looked around the courtyard for another option, then pointed to a stack of mud-bricks beside the kitchen wall.

"We can rearrange those bricks, lay Asher on them, and prepare him there. First, we need to change, or these clothes will be ruined."

Once they changed into robes that could be discarded afterwards, Miriam went into the room again while Esther and Rachel moved the stack of mud-bricks so they could lay Asher full-length. The awful smell still stained the air in the room, but it didn't seem so bad. Miriam suspected she was getting used to the odor,

Miriam feared Asher's body would be in that stiff stage where none of his limbs could be moved. She kneeled beside the mattress, moved the thin blanket to one side, and lifted his arm. Asher's arm came up easily and with no resistance.

Miriam released a sigh of relief. Either the stiffness had passed, or not yet come upon Asher. Either way meant they could prepare the body more easily.

"How will we move him?" Rachel asked from the doorway.

Miriam let the blanket fall back, swallowed hard. She had glimpsed enough of the damage to Asher's body to confirm her fear she would not like what was under the blanket.

"It feels wrong to carry him out with his arms and legs hanging loosely," she said.

"Why not leave him on the mattress? We can pull it out to the bricks, and lift him from there." Esther had leaned her head through the door, nose wrinkling. "And we should wrap a wet cloth across our mouth and nose. It will help mask the smell."

"I have rosemary oil in my bag," Miriam said, pushing to her feet. "A few drops on the cloth will also help."

The straw mattress seemed to have a mind of its own. The sharp ends of the straw stabbed at their fingers, and when they pushed the mattress toward the door, it caught and twisted, threatening to tip Asher's body onto the floor.

"We are doing this the wrong way," Miriam said as another attempt to move the mattress failed.

She pulled the cloth from her face, wiped her forehead, and pushed strands of hair away from her eyes. She pushed to her feet and walked outside. It didn't feel any cooler in the open air, but at least she could breathe deeply.

"We could try working in the room," Esther said from the doorway. Her face was flushed, and she breathed heavily, almost wheezing.

Miriam shook her head as an idea came to her. "You were right the first time. We would be ill or passed out in a short time. Let's all be on the same side of the mattress and line it up with the doorway."

The suggestion worked.

Soon after, they had the mattress aligned with the doorway. Miriam guided the end near Asher's head, while Esther and Rachel pulled the mattress through the doorway and out into the open. At one point, the mattress cloth snagged and ripped, and the last few paces to bring the mattress alongside the stack of bricks left a trail of straw spilled in a ragged line on the ground.

Miriam bent down and carefully lifted the blanket off Asher's body.

Beside her, Esther made a soft noise and turned away. Miriam glanced at Rachel, saw her face was pale, her eyes wide with horror.

Miriam looked down again at Asher's body and feared she was going to be sick. She knew enough about the body to know the wounds and bruises had been inflicted to cause the most amount of pain.

She lay the blanket over the bricks and said. "I'll lift his head and shoulders, Esther, you take his waist, and Rachel his feet. We'll cut the binding ropes once he's settled. Ready?"

The other two women nodded in assent, readied themselves and on Miriam's command, lifted Asher and placed him on the blanket.

"Be grateful this isn't Isaac," Esther said. "We'd never have got him off the ground."

Rachel giggled, then clamped her hand over her mouth, a flush spreading over her thin cheeks. "I'm sorry."

"Don't apologize," Miriam said. "On the few occasions I met Asher, he was a man who enjoyed life. I think he would have laughed as you did."

"I saw nothing like this during the fall of Jerusalem, and there are sights from that time I will never forget," Esther said. She shook her head, looking at the wounds on Asher's body like she didn't quite believe what she was seeing.

"Who would do this to another person?"

"I don't know who and neither does Jacob," Miriam said. "The why is easy. Whoever did this believed Asher had information they wanted."

"Information about what?" Rachel asked as she pulled cloths and jars from her bag and arranged them on the bricks beside Asher's body.

"Something else I don't know," Miriam said. "We can ask Jacob when he arrives. Let's get water from the well and begin preparing, Asher."

As they worked, Miriam recited what she could remember from the psalms of Tahara. She began with a psalm of Moses, letting her voice fall into the cadence of the chant she had heard so many times in the Temple in Jerusalem.

"May the pleasantness of the Lord be upon us; establish for us the work of our hands; establish the work of our hands."

From there, she changed to a psalm of King David, and then another by Moses. Esther and Rachel joined her in the chant as they recognized the words.

It took nearly an hour to finish washing the blood and grime from Asher's body, clean the wounds, straighten the broken nose, and realign the twisted ankle.

"Enough for the moment while his body dries," Miriam said. She stood straight, pushing her knuckles into the small of her back where a dull ache had begun.

"I brought a full wineskin with me, and I think we deserve a rest before the purification. The worst heat of the day is gone and it will be easier now."

They completed the purification and were laying out the white shroud Rachel provided when Miriam heard the crunch of footsteps on the stone pathway leading to the road along the far side of the orchard.

She looked up, saw Jacob, and was surprised to see Ligish with him.

"I came to help," Ligish said as he stripped his tunic off and accepted the shovel Jacob handed him. The two men exchanged a few words, and Ligish set off back the way they had come.

Jacob came toward Miriam, and she realized he was carrying a small bundle.

She wiped her hands on a cloth and stepped away from Asher's body so as not to impede Esther and Rachel.

He looks tired and worn, Miriam thought as Jacob reached her. Even more than he did this morning. She guessed his visit with Arioch had not gone well.

"Isaac and Samuel will be here before sundown, and we will bury him then." Jacob said. "After, we will go to Samuel's house. This is for Asher." He offered her the bundle, and as she took the weight in her hands, she realized what it was.

"Your prayer shawl?"

He nodded. "I have no time to find where Asher's belongings are stored. This will give him a piece of Judah."

The lamb's wool was soft on her hands, worn thin in places so you could see through it. She had repaired several sections for him in the last years, and the original white color had faded to a dirty cream.

"I'll make you a new one," she said.

He looked about to say something, shook his head, and swallowed hard. His voice was hoarse. "Ligish and I found a good place to lay Asher. It won't take us long to prepare his grave."

Miriam nodded. Unable to trust herself to talk, she reached for his hand, squeezed his fingers. He returned the pressure, released her.

She had already begun working on a new shawl for Jacob. Something she planned to give him when they married.

Miriam watched him as he walked away, following Ligish into the orchard, and promised herself the new shawl would not wait for their wedding.

It was an hour later; the sun slipping below the walls of Babylon behind them, when Jacob and Ligish returned with Isaac and Samuel beside them. The men were sweaty, dusty, and dirty after digging the grave.

Miriam watched as Jacob stacked the shovels, then went to the well and pulled up a pail of clean water.

She smiled at the look on Ligish's face. He shook his head and said. "If you ever invite me here when the house is finished, Jacob, I will refuse. If my wife sees what you've done here, I will never hear the last."

Miriam felt a smile tug at her face as Rachel laughed, the musical notes lifting the somber feeling. "I told Miriam the same thing about Samuel."

Jacob shrugged. There was a soft smile on his face. "If it means Miriam and I have quiet and peaceful evenings together, then it's a sacrifice I'm prepared to make."

The smile disappeared, and he became serious.

"The sun is getting lower. We men will carry Asher on the blanket."

With one of them on each corner, it was a quick and short journey through the almond orchard to the grave Jacob and Ligish had prepared.

Miriam walked between Esther and Rachel, the three of them silent as they watched Jacob and Ligish lift Asher carefully from the blanket into his last resting place.

When Asher's body was settled in the shallow grave, Miriam linked her hands with Esther on her left and Rachel on her right.

There was a silence between the three of them. In a detached way Miriam realized the birds had also fallen quiet, like they understood and respected the occasion. She waited a moment longer, then squeezed the hands of the other women.

Together, they said. "Asher, son of Jonathan. We ask forgiveness from you if we did not treat you respectfully, but we did, as is our custom. May you be a messenger for all of Judah. Go in peace, rest in peace, and arise in your turn at the end of days."

There was silence, then Jacob said. "We always hope our last resting place is in Judah. I regret I cannot give you that honor, Asher. Or place the earth of our homeland with your shroud."

He looked like he was about to say more, put his hand over his mouth and shook his head.

Miriam glanced at Isaac, who gave a tiny shake of his head. It surprised her when Ligish spoke, his voice thick with emotion.

"I know your tradition is to bury someone with nothing, so all are equal in the eyes of your God. In the brief time I knew Asher, he became a good and trusted friend.

"With your permission, Jacob, I want to leave Asher with a token of my god, Marduk. We do not know what waits for us beyond, and I would like to give him every advantage."

Miriam looked at Jacob on the opposite side of the grave. His face was closed. It was one of the few times she couldn't guess what he was thinking.

She realized everyone else was looking at Jacob. As she watched, his face twisted into a smile.

"If for no other reason than it would irritate our priests, I would say yes. More important to me is I want to give my friend, our friend, every advantage wherever he is. Please, Ligish, give Asher whatever tokens you believe will help him."

Ligish went down on one knee, leaned over the grave, and pulled two silver tokens from the pocket of his tunic. He placed them gently on the shroud, about where Asher's chest would be. "Thank you," he said.

When Ligish regained his place, Jacob bent down and gripped the edge of the blanket.

Miriam nudged Esther and Rachel aside, squatted, and gripped the edges of the blanket on her side of the grave.

It wasn't tradition, but so much of today had broken those rules, and this was about Asher, not what the priests said.

Jacob lifted his side of the blanket, shaking pieces of dirt off and folding it over Asher's body. When he was done, Miriam repeated the actions on her side, providing a double layer of coverage. She focused her attention on making the blanket fall smoothly, and not allowing herself to be distracted by the figure she glimpsed watching them from the road.

When Miriam was done, she rose to her feet, stepped back, and allowed the men to fill the grave. She breathed deeply, letting the nutty, woody aroma of the almonds fill her body.

"Our house is close by," Rachel said as the men finished. "We have wine and food, and it will be right to talk of Asher. He had no family here, so we will be his family. That includes you, Ligish."

"It will be an honor to join you for a short time," Ligish said to Rachel.

Then, in a low voice, Miriam could barely hear, he said to Jacob. "Meet me at Bel Ibni's house tomorrow afternoon. We have much to discuss."

Miriam watched as he moved away to introduce himself to Samuel Jacob came up beside her. "I saw him too," he said.

Miriam looked down to the road again, watched with Jacob as the figure turned, walked slowly away toward the Marduk Gate.

"I'm not sure that was a man," she said.

CHAPTER FIVE

The fifth day of Abu - Late Morning

The heat of the previous day had continued into the morning. Jacob wore a sleeveless tunic as he made his way along the dusty road beside the irrigation canals to the north of Babylon.

It was a longer walk to the Sin Gate than using the Marduk Gate on the eastern side of the city, but Jacob preferred it. Smaller, and less busy than the larger, more popular Ishtar and Marduk Gates, the Sin Gate let him enter and leave the Inner City with shorter lines and fewer people.

The guards were inspecting a cart carrying six waist-high ceramic jars when Jacob arrived at the gate. The gate commander, a veteran who walked with a limp and had streaks of gray and silver through his hair and beard, recognized Jacob, and waved him past the inspection.

Jacob's destination was a tavern two streets from the Sin Gate. The tavern stood on the corner of an alley where the mud brick on the houses flaked away and strips of ragged cloth instead of animal hide covered the doorways.

There was no covering over the doorway to the tavern. Jacob stepped through and down a step, blinking his eyes in the dim smoky interior. Two of the tables were occupied with men who talked quietly and shared large jugs of beer. They looked like laborers taking a break in the heat of the day and making it last as long as possible before having to leave.

A serving girl came toward him as he weaved between the tables toward a booth in the corner. Jacob didn't recognize her and guessed she was new.

"I'll take the booth in the corner, a beer, and Gideon's company," he said.

"I'm not sure Gideon is here," she said, keeping her head down so her dark hair hung over her face, not meeting his look.

"He's in the kitchen counting the copper and silver from last night. Tell him Jacob's here."

Her head came up, dark eyes wide. Her mouth had dropped open in an "o" of surprise.

She nodded and scurried away.

Jacob had barely settled on the cushions in the booth when the serving girl returned and placed a jug of beer and two tankards on the table.

"You must stop frightening my people," Gideon said as he slid onto the bench opposite Jacob and filled the tankards.

Gideon was a slender man about the same height as Jacob. His face looked carved from stone, his arms corded with muscle.

Jacob had spent the journey from Samuel's house wrestling with the best way to give Gideon the news. He could find no easy way, had never found one when telling families during the siege of Jerusalem.

In a low voice, he said. "I buried Asher yesterday."

Gideon had the tankard half-way to his mouth. His arm stopped. Carefully, he lowered the tankard down to the table. In the flickering light of the sesame oil lamp, his face was hard, unmoving. Jacob had seen the slight tremor in Gideon's hand when he put down the tankard, and the flicker of pain in Gideon's eyes.

"When you came through the door, I sensed you had bad news for me, Jacob. What happened?"

"He was left near the house I'm building outside the city walls. Whoever it was knew I was sleeping there."

"Any idea who?"

Jacob shook his head, his throat suddenly dry. He took a long drink from his own tankard. "I suggested him to Ligish maybe two moons ago. He was trying to find out who is behind the thefts and other incidents at the Esagila."

"I'd say he found them," Gideon said, then after a pause. "He was the last one, wasn't he?"

Jacob nodded, not trusting himself to speak.

There were six of them originally. The first special team created by the generals in the Judean army. They were trained to infiltrate behind the Babylonian lines and cause as much disruption as possible.

Only Jacob and Asher had survived to reach Babylon.

Jacob shook his head. He would always see their faces in his mind. And now Asher's bloodied, beaten, and broken had joined them.

"Ligish told me he met Asher here several times. Have you seen or heard anything?"

"Not about this. The first time I saw them together, Asher acted like he didn't know me, so I left them alone. There is something that may help you. Wait here."

Gideon edged out of the booth. He was gone for several minutes. When he returned, he handed Jacob a small papyrus scroll about as long as his hand from fingertips to wrist.

"Asher came to see me six, maybe seven, days ago," Gideon said. "He was alone and gave me that scroll. He insisted I give this to you if anything happened to him."

"Did he say what he was doing or where he was going?"

Gideon shook his head. "No, and I didn't ask him. He looked tense though, unsettled, maybe a little scared."

Asher scared?

The thought sent a shiver through Jacob's body. He hadn't known Asher was capable of fear.

Jacob turned the scroll over in his hands, feeling the rough edges scrape against the skin of his palms. He studied the strips of papyrus that bound the scroll and the wax seal, keeping everything closed. The piece of wax was smooth, no symbols or writing on it. He wouldn't expect Asher to leave marks or symbols that could be recognized or traced.

Jacob squeezed the scroll with his right hand and cracked the seal. He eased his fingers under the broken wax and teased the edges free.

Using both hands, he unrolled the scroll, then turned it sideways so he could read the message Asher had left for him. The message was brief, just over ten words.

And not at all what he expected.

"You look shocked," Gideon said.

Jacob passed him the scroll. They'd had very few secrets in Jerusalem.

Fewer now.

"Asher had a woman?"

Gideon smiled at him. "Why not? You have Miriam."

"You never met her? The woman. I know you've met Miriam."

Gideon waved his arm to take in the interior of the inn behind them. "You don't bring Miriam here unless you have to, and I don't blame you. I never met her, and Asher never told me. I suspected he was involved with a woman. I didn't know her name was Debra until you gave me the scroll."

Jacob felt a pang of something in his chest. It took him a few moments to recognize it and understand where it came from.

Anger.

Anger at Asher for not telling him.

Anger at Gideon as well, for suspecting, and not telling him. Jacob struggled to keep his voice low and even.

"You knew about her? Debra."

Gideon shook his head. "Suspected, I said. I was going to ask him the day he left the scroll for you, but he was too distracted. I didn't want to add to his stress by asking a question he may have wanted to avoid."

Jacob nodded. It made sense, and no point continuing to be angry at Gideon.

He held out his hand, took the scroll back from Gideon, and read the words again. The symbols were formed carefully and precisely, exactly the way Asher always wrote.

Jacob leaned forward, sniffing at the scroll. There was no smell of limes, just the dry odor of crushed reeds. To be certain, he held the scroll beside the flame of the sesame oil lamp. Not too close, but close enough to warm the papyrus and highlight anything written with lime juice and invisible without the heat of the lamp to bring it out.

There was nothing.

"He calls her Debra here," Jacob said. "Nothing else, and no way for me to find her."

"Perhaps she is supposed to find you. Do you know where Asher lived?"

"He lived in the army camp at Borsippa. The army wouldn't allow a woman inside the encampment. Not officially, anyway. As a foreigner, Asher wouldn't risk his position in that way. If he had another home, he never told me about it."

"Maybe it's her home we should look for," Gideon said.

"And how many women named Debra are there in Babylon and the surrounding villages? It's a popular name among our people, and one the Babylonians like to use as well."

"You could ask our priests."

Jacob picked up his tankard and gave Gideon what he hoped was a glare. "I'll assume you intended that to be humorous," Jacob said. Gideon knew Jacob's opinion of the Judean priests, shared it most of the time.

"She may be safer where she is, rather than coming to me."

"Possibly," Gideon said. He refilled their tankards, then changed the subject. "How bad is this ban Arioch has imposed?"

Jacob sipped at his beer, not surprised Gideon knew of the ban. He let the bubbles and tart flavor roll over his tongue. Gideon was working on recreating the richer, darker beers of Judah. This was better than the thin watery brews most Babylonians served, but it still had too much of a tart flavor for Jacob's liking.

"It will cripple Isaac, Bel Ibni, and myself if the ban remains in force for long. It will also destroy the goodwill all of us Judeans have earned with the other merchants and tamkurum in Babylon and the other cities."

Gideon shook his head. "What caused it? Arioch doesn't normally do the bidding of the anti-Judean voices."

"I caused it," Jacob said, still feeling the sting of Arioch's words.

"I thought I was being clever by sending a fast caravan to Nineveh and securing their wine harvests for the next two seasons. Arioch sees it differently, even though he gets the major portion of the wine. I still have to tell Bel Ibni, and find a way for us all to survive this, although sitting here drinking your beer is a much more attractive idea."

"It won't solve anything, Jacob. It never does."

Jacob allowed himself a smile at his friend's words. "Knowledge we both got the hard way."

He took a long drink of the beer, then said. "Arioch also threatened to confiscate everything that comes back with the Judah caravan. If he does, I'll be begging for scraps on the streets of Kweiresh."

"I doubt you'll be begging for anything," Gideon said. He tipped the jug to refill Jacob's beer, scowled when he realized the jug was empty. He leaned round the curtain and called to a server.

"You'll come up with something. You always do, and you might even find the people Asher was looking for."

"That's the first requirement Arioch has before he'll consider removing the bans. I think finding this Debra will be a start. You're sure Asher said nothing about her, anything about what he learned?" Jacob lifted his hand in response to the spark that flashed in Gideon's eyes.

"I know. You already told me, but this was Asher. Please, Gideon, think again."

"You're right."

Gideon folded his arms across his chest, sat back, closed his eyes, and seemed to fold into himself.

He didn't react when the server placed a fresh foaming jug on the table, or when Jacob refilled both their tankards.

Finally, Gideon opened his eyes, sat forward, and drank from his tankard.

"My guess is Asher met her after he started working for Ligish. Based on the way he wrote her name, our way, not the Babylonian way, she's most likely Judean. Consider that the most likely option, not a reality."

Jacob thought about Gideon's words as he sipped at his beer. "The timing makes me suspicious. Could she have been sent as a distraction by the people Asher was looking for?"

"The timing concerns me as well," Gideon said as they both pushed to their feet.

"Be very careful, Jacob. I like Miriam. Don't make her a widow before you're married."

CHAPTER SIX

The fifth day of Abu - Afternoon

It was early afternoon before Miriam convinced both Rachel and Esther she would be perfectly safe, making the brief journey alone to the house Jacob was building. The previous day they had bundled the cloths, and rags used to prepare Asher's body into a pile, and left them. Miriam wanted to clean up and burn the rags, so there was nothing left to attract rats or other vermin.

Miriam had also promised to return to Rachel's house in time for the evening prayers. She understood their concern, but she really, really wanted some time to herself.

She paused at the piece of stone Jacob had used to mark Asher's grave. Jacob intended to replace the stone with a more permanent and properly carved marker once he had time to commission the work.

The sun had passed its zenith and was behind her now. The almond trees cast shadows over the grave and made the heat seem a little less oppressive.

Miriam paused at the graveside, grateful for the shade, and ready for a brief rest before making her way up the slight slope to the part-built house. She lowered the clay fire pot, with embers from Rachel's kitchen fire, to the ground, and adjusted the bag on her shoulder.

She studied the stone, thought about the man laid to rest there, and said. "I wish we'd known each other better, Asher. I know how much you meant to Jacob. He will avenge you, but I suspect you already know that."

Miriam wanted to add something more, but no words seemed adequate. She gave a nod to the grave, adjusted her bag again, then spotted the blanket they had used to bring Asher from the house to his final resting place.

She bent down, bundled the blanket into her arms. Her nose wrinkled at the smell of dried blood and the sharp, bitter tang of the oils used to cleanse and purify Asher's body.

She ignored the smell, picked up the fire pot and made her way up the slope to the house.

As she had expected, the fire in the partly constructed kitchen was a pile of cold gray ashes. Miriam placed the blanket and her bag by the wall and went to the fireplace. The heat in the ashes was from the sun, not from any embers. She used a shovel to clear the ashes from the fireplace, keeping her breathing shallow to avoid the gray ash dust that rose and floated around her as she worked.

Miriam offered a prayer of thanks to Jacob when she saw the neatly stacked piles of wood on the far side of the kitchen. She selected some thin strips of palm, and some larger logs that smelled like mesquite, and re-stacked them by the fireplace.

Carefully, Miriam lifted the lid from the fire pot, tipped the hot coals onto the ground where she had cleared the ashes, rearranged the coals into a small pile, and added the thin strips of palm. After a few moments, thin threads of smoke curled up from the wood. She blew gently on the coals until the first spikes of orange flame appeared.

Palm burned quickly and with little heat. As the flames became larger, Miriam added more wood to the fire, arranging the mesquite and thin pieces of palm side by side with gaps between for the air to flow.

Leaving the fire to gain strength, Miriam collected the loose straw and piled it onto the remains of the mattress. The cloths had dried overnight, and she put them in a separate pile with the remains of Asher's ripped and bloodied clothes.

The straw and the cloth mattress cover burned fiercely. Miriam soaked the blanket and cloths with sesame oil from a jug in her bag, and added them to the flames, stepping back as the oil flared and sent a wall of nutty sesame smelling heat over her.

She watched the fire for a few minutes, making sure it didn't burn out of control, or spit sparks and embers to start another blaze.

Satisfied the fire was safe, Miriam walked across the courtyard to the side of the house that had full walls and a roof. The inside smelled of damp mud and clay and had more light than she expected. Isaac's house in the Inner City was one of a long row of connected buildings. The few windows in Isaac's house looked out onto the courtyard and let in very little light.

Here, Jacob had left large openings that allowed light to come into the room. With no coverings, the window openings also allowed in the heat, which seemed more intense than outside. Her father's house in Jerusalem had been too hot in the summer, and too cold in the winter. She would talk to Jacob about that. A well-built house should be cool on the inside to protect everyone from the heat of summer days like this one.

She glanced behind to check on the fire. Reassured there were no problems, Miriam crossed the room to the archway that led along a passageway. Three openings on her left led into more rooms. Two were the same size, the third much larger. She remembered from her talks with Jacob this would be the room where she and Jacob slept.

A shiver of anticipation rippled through her body as her mind leaped to the thought of their wedding night.

Miriam shook her head.

Only a prophet could suggest when that might be. Isaac had agreed for them to be married on the second Sabbath after the return of the Judah caravan. There had been no news of the caravan in over two moons.

She wondered what would happen if the caravan never returned, then dismissed the thought. Asher's death had caused enough problems. There was no sense in adding to them.

As she retraced her steps to the main room, Miriam realized the house would need furniture and rugs and wall-hangings. There had been no opportunity for her to add any personal touch to the house she entered when she married priest Nahum. His house was established as he wanted it. She learned the hard way he would tolerate no changes.

Miriam felt another shiver of anticipation. Excitement this time. Jacob had a small house in the Inner City. Even if he moved everything to this house, it would need many more rugs and wall-hangings.

She went back to the large bedroom, paced out the dimensions, and did the same for the other bedrooms, thinking about what she wanted to put in each room.

Miriam squinted as she came out into the bright light. When her eyes adjusted, she checked the fire. The flames had died down, leaving a bed of glowing embers. She was relieved to see most of the linens and cloths had burned to ash, and used a piece of wood to push the remaining fragments onto the embers where they sent up plumes of smoke that got in her eyes and throat, and made her cough.

She shuffled back, doubled over with the coughing, eyes streaming, hand waving before her face to clear away the remnants of the smoke. When the coughing subsided, Miriam wiped her sleeve across her eyes, stood straight, saw a flicker of movement in the orchard.

She made a point of wiping her eyes again, taking a few steps away from, and to one side of, the fire. She didn't look directly at the trees, just used her side vision to get a sense of what was in the shadows.

It took a while before she saw the flicker of movement again.

This time, she was certain.

Miriam couldn't tell what it was, just saw a darker shadow among the shadows cast by the branches and leaves.

A shadow that moved against the way the wind was blowing. It moved slowly and carefully, enough that not even the birds objected to the movement.

There was someone in the orchard.

For the first time, Miriam questioned her desire to be alone this afternoon, and regretted not strapping the bone sewing needle to her left forearm. The needle had saved her life two moons ago, and keeping it on her body had become a habit.

Miriam fanned her hand before her face again, making it look like she was still suffering from the smoke. She studied the fire, and the surrounding ground, then bent over again, making hacking coughing noises.

When she was doubled over, Miriam snatched a sliver of wood about as thick as two of her fingers and twice the length of her hand from the edge of the pile. She held it close to her chest as she stood upright.

Miriam walked to the edge of the courtyard with more confidence than she felt. She studied the trees and shadows, not seeing anything odd, wondered if she had imagined the movement, then discarded the thought.

"I know you're in the trees," Miriam called out. "There's nothing here worth stealing. Come out. Tell me why you're here, and what you want."

For a long moment, it seemed Miriam was talking to herself. Then she saw movement in the shadows, a crunching of twigs and small branches that set the birds squawking and fluttering away in a rush and flurry of flapping wings.

A figure in a dark hooded robe picked its way out of the trees and stopped at the edge of the courtyard.

Miriam remembered the figure she and Jacob had seen the previous day.

"Who are you?" Miriam asked. She made no attempt to hide the way she held the piece of wood.

The person pushed the hood back off her head, revealing the face of a young woman, maybe twenty summers old. As the hood slid back, night-black hair tumbled free, down over her shoulders. Her eyes were as dark as her hair, her face narrow with high cheekbones. She clasped her hands in front of her, one kneading the other.

"Who are you?" Miriam said again, letting a hint of impatience into her tone. "What are you doing here?"

The woman dropped her gaze then, looked at a point on the ground just in front of Miriam's feet.

Her voice was a soft croak, like she wasn't used to speaking. Miriam couldn't place her accent.

"Asher told me to find Jacob, then I saw the stone. It's him, isn't it? It's Asher, isn't it? He's buried there."

"What's your name?" Miriam said.

A long pause.

"Deborah," the woman said finally. "Debra."

CHAPTER SEVEN

The fifth day of Abu - Afternoon

It was a walk of a few minutes south along Sin Street from Gideon's inn to the large house Bel Ibni owned on the edge of the Kullab ward in the Inner City. The house was three streets from where Sin Street joined the major thoroughfare of Marduk Street. There was a constant background of chatter, braying animals, and the rumble of cartwheels from both busy streets.

It was too much noise for Jacob. His own house was to the north and east, in the New Town ward, close to the city walls and away from busy streets. It occurred to him as he walked he needed to decide whether to keep the house n the quiet street, or let it go, and spend all his time in the house he was building.

The beer he had drunk with Gideon didn't make the decision any easier until he realized Miriam should have her thoughts heard as well. That meant he didn't have to decide yet, and there was a smile on his face as he reached the front of Bel Ibni's house.

Bel Ibni's door guard, Huba, waved a gnarled hand in greeting. As a boy, Huba had served Bel Ibni's grandfather. When he had the time,

Jacob enjoyed sitting with the old man, listening to the stories Huba told of his younger years.

"On the roof."

Huba gestured for Jacob to go into the house and settled back into the dark niche that provided a cool refuge from the scorching afternoon.

Jacob went through the short passageway into the inner courtyard. The air in the courtyard was still, the heat searing at Jacob's nose and throat as he breathed. He crossed the courtyard quickly and made his way up the steps leading to the roof.

Bel Ibni had strengthened the ceilings of the house and built a terrace where a bare roof had once been. A beige awning shaded the terrace and flapped lazily in the light wind. It was much cooler up here than on the streets.

Jacob was considering building something similar in the new house, but hadn't decided if it was really worth the extra time and cost.

As he reached the top of the stairs, he realized it was something else to discuss with Miriam, again not a decision for today. And that made him smile once more.

The beige awning stretched all the way across the open space, providing shade for a table and three long couches. A flagon of wine, goblets, and plates of nuts and fruits filled the table.

Bel Ibni sprawled on one of the couches, and it seemed to Jacob the Babylonian merchant had gained more weight since they had last seen each other. Beside Bel Ibni, on a second couch, was a man dressed in a sleeveless tunic of rough cloth and trews stained, patched and torn.

It was only when the man turned his head and Jacob saw the dark brown eyes; he realized it was Ligish.

"There are too many eyes and ears at the Esagila," Ligish said. "It seemed prudent to appear as someone else, so there was less chance of being followed."

Jacob nodded in agreement as he reached the table. He dropped onto the couch opposite Ligish, reached for the jug of wine, and poured a small amount into a goblet. After the beer he had drunk with Gideon, he needed to keep his head clear.

"Have you told Bel Ibni about the ban on permits?"

"He has," Bel Ibni said, wriggling on the couch so he could sit upright. "I'm not happy with it, but I doubt there's anything we can do until you find the people who killed your friend, Asher."

"There isn't," Ligish said with a shake of his head. "I've only seen Arioch this stubborn once or twice, but when he gets this way, there's no moving him."

"I'm sure the Nineveh business didn't help his mood," Jacob said, then turned to Bel Ibni. "I thought I was being clever, but Arioch didn't see it that way."

Bel Ibni shrugged, poured himself a large helping of wine from the jug. "A miscalculation, Jacob, nothing more. I made many over the years, some of them you helped me fix."

A good mouthful of wine drained from his cup. As it was some of the wine he'd brought back from Nineveh, Jacob allowed himself another, more generous measure.

"I didn't expect you to be so understanding," he said.

Bel Ibni shrugged again. "It's not something aimed at just you and me, so everyone suffers equally. And, I believe Damkina is with child, so at the moment, I'm seeing nothing but good in the world."

Jacob sipped at his wine, did some quick calculations in his head. The wedding of Bel Ibni's son, Horam, to Damkina, was just over two moons ago.

"It must have been quite the wedding night," he said, and Bel Ibni laughed.

"So it must, and thank Marduk, the astrologers made correct predictions. Let's see if they are right about the child being a boy."

"That itself is worth a thanksgiving sacrifice," Ligish said. "It's early for her as yet. I'll add my prayers that all goes well for them both."

He took a mouthful of wine and his face became serious.

"You want to know more about what Asher was doing for us?"

"I need as many details as possible," Jacob said. "Start with those you suspect, both inside and outside the Esagila."

"I should give you some privacy," Bel Ibni said, and began struggling to his feet.

"If Jacob has no objections, I would like you to stay," Ligish said.

"You may have insights into some of these people that go beyond what I know, or suspect."

"I don't mind," Jacob said. "The more help from people I trust, the better."

He sat forward on the couch, said to Ligish. "When we talked about this before you recruited Asher, I asked who in the Esagila wanted to replace Arioch. You said everyone."

"I did," Ligish said. "It was an exaggeration. Arioch is well liked. He could be High Priest if he put his mind to it, but he refuses to play games with the King and the court. I don't blame him, although I believe he'd make an excellent High Priest."

"Subisha doesn't believe him," Bel Ibni said. "Subisha considers it an act."

Ligish smiled, but there was no humor in it. "Subisha wants to be High Priest. He wants it badly, and he sees Arioch as his chief rival."

"I've heard of Subisha," Jacob said. "I've never met him. What does he do for the Esagila?"

"Subisha handles all the grain and livestock we manage. When grain, promised to the temple in Erech, was spoiled, it was Subisha, I suspected. Arioch and I looked hard, but found nothing to connect Subisha with that incident."

"He's hard but fair," Bel Ibni said. "The shepherds and goat herders have respect for him. It's also well known, Subisha desires to be High Priest, but you're unlikely to actually meet him. Subisha's chief clerk, Makru, is very protective." He looked up at the awning, flapping gently as the air moved, a slight frown on his forehead as he considered something.

"It was six years ago," he said finally. "Maybe seven. Before we conquered Jerusalem and you Judeans arrived. We had a drought that year, and no amount of sacrifices to Marduk or any of the other gods made a difference. Subisha worked day and night to help those men and help save their herds. I can see him stealing the silver and olibanum at the New Year, but not spoiling grain that might have been used to feed the herds. There's a belief, and I've heard it said, that Subisha cares more about the animals than he does people."

"I was on campaign in Lebanon and heard the same story about the drought. It was just before Subisha promoted Makru," Ligish said.

"There are others who would like to be High Priest, or have Arioch's position, but none have enough of a following to be considered seriously."

"Do any of those priests have alliances with the merchants?" Jacob asked.

Ligish shrugged, and shook his head, then looked to Bel Ibni and picked some dates from the platter on the table. "Possibly. That was something Asher was working on."

"Are you here to share information, or as an officer of the Esagila?" Bel Ibni asked, and Jacob heard the tension in his voice.

"Share information," Ligish said without hesitation.

The hunch of Bel Ibni's shoulders relaxed. "It's a dangerous game, trying to build alliances with priests. My father did it once, and it nearly destroyed us. Since then, I've tried to keep away from it." He took a long swallow of wine, as if the speech had left him parched.

"Damkina's father, Rimut, has an arrangement with one of the junior priests who is under Arioch," he raised his hand before Ligish could say anything. "I don't know who it is, and if I did, I wouldn't tell you."

"I understand," Ligish said. "What of the others?"

Bel Ibni added several names to the list. Jacob recognized all of them, had done business with some. The fourth name Bel Ibni mentioned made Jacob sit a little straighter, pay more attention.

"I thought Nurval had strong connections with Sin, your goddess of the Moon," he said.

"He does," Ligish said. "He is also a frequent visitor to the Esagila, always private, and supposedly with Iddin. I made some discrete inquiries. Everyone I spoke with acknowledges the presence of Nurval, but no-one admits to seeing Iddin."

Or the people questioned were more afraid of their master than they were of Ligish and Arioch, Jacob thought.

Jacob knew Iddin well; both by reputation and personally.

Although he made a living as a reasonably successful merchant, most of Iddin's income and wealth came from gambling and prostitution. Their paths had crossed twice. Jacob still considered himself lucky to have survived both encounters without harm or injury.

The wounds on Asher's body were consistent with what Jacob had seen of Iddin's methods.

Once again, Jacob saw, in his mind, the bloodied damage to his friend, felt the slow burn of anger flare in his gut. He took another sip of wine, kept his voice even.

"If I had to make a choice, I would look first at Iddin."

"My choice as well," Ligish said with a grim smile. "That's where Asher started, but he found nothing. It appears Iddin is aware of his reputation in the city, and that it will impact the chances of a good match for any of his three daughters."

"I heard the same," Bel Ibni said. "There was an approach to me about Horam. My son was already betrothed to Damkina, so I could decline in a more polite way than I believe some others responded."

"What does influence in the Esagila gain him?" Jacob asked.

"Respectability," Ligish and Bel Ibni said at the same time.

The two men smiled briefly.

Ligish twirled the wine goblet in his fingers, then said. "Iddin is trying to step away from his more unsavory activities. Cultivating the right relationships within the temple of Marduk, and the Esagila allows him to represent himself as a reformed person."

Jacob thought about the implications for a moment, decided he would find out how serious, and how successful, Iddin was at distancing himself from those unsavory activities.

He looked across to Bel Ibni. "We became distracted by Iddin. Tell me more about Nurval. Other than his preference for Sin, the goddess of the Moon, I recall he trades mostly to the east, with the Elamites, the Medes, and the Achaemenids. I know little else."

"He spends as little time in Babylon as he can," Bel Ibni said. "Most of his visits are to the Esagila to pay respects. I don't know where he stays when he's in Babylon. His main house is in the city of Haran, close to the temple of the Moon."

"Nurval's wife is a distant relative of King Nebuchadnezzar," Ligish said. "They stay at the palace when they travel to Babylon, although Nurval spends most of his time with his people on the caravan grounds. Many of the nobles frown on those of you who make a living as merchants. I think the disapproval makes Nurval uncomfortable."

"The same as in Jerusalem," Jacob said. He pushed to his feet. "I'll see if I can find Nurval on the caravan grounds. How will I recognize him?"

"You won't be able to miss him," Ligish said. "Nurval is tall. One of the tallest men I've ever seen. Asher said he could be a Nephilim."

"A what?" Bel Ibni asked.

"A race of giants, or large men, who, legend says, lived in Israel and Judah at the time of Noah and after," Jacob said.

"He looks large only because he's so much taller than most other men," Ligish said. "He wears pale colors to honor Sin, the Moon goddess. If he's at the caravan grounds, you won't miss him."

"You've both given me much to consider," Jacob said, and stepped carefully between the couches.

"Let me think on this tonight, and I will plan my approach tomorrow. How do I contact you without drawing attention to either of us, Ligish?"

"Asher had an arrangement with Gideon," Ligish said. "Let's continue to use that. Today is the fifth day of Abu. Let's meet there late in the morning of the eighth day."

As he left Bel Ibni's house, with another gesture of acknowledgment to Huba, Jacob offered a prayer of thanks that he had sipped small amounts of wine.

Ligish and Bel Ibni had given him much to think about. He wanted to talk with Gideon, but the direct link Gideon claimed to the Esagila had surprised Jacob, made him more cautious.

As he walked toward his home in the New Town ward of the city, Jacob wondered if his old spymaster was reassessing loyalties.

CHAPTER EIGHT

The fifth day of Abu - Evening

Miriam settled herself in a chair on the balcony outside the small room she had in Isaac's home. The balcony ran the length of the second story of the house, with steps at the far end leading down into the courtyard where Isaac's sons chattered and played together.

The chair gave a creak of protest as Miriam moved to open the part-finished shawl she had begun for Jacob. She had commissioned the main part of the shawl from a friend of Isaacs, using the finest lamb's wool she could find in exchange for some of her best salves and tonics.

Miriam had insisted she would add the strings for the tzitzit herself. It was a skill she learned at an early age, sitting beside her mother and separating the eight strands, tying the five knots on each strand.

It was only after her mother died that Miriam learned the significance of the eight strands and five knots. Combined with the number the priests assigned to the word tzitzit, the result came to the number six hundred and thirteen, a reminder of the number of Commandments in the Laws.

There was still enough light for her to make some progress, perhaps another strand or two of knots if she concentrated.

The white lamb's wool was soft under her fingers. She let her hands lay still on the shawl, while her mind replayed everything she had done since seeing the woman, Debra.

So much for concentration.

It had been with reluctance that Miriam had left Debra with Rachel and Samuel. She had really wanted to bring Debra either to Isaac's home, or to Jacob's house in the Inner City. When she suggested it, Debra became flustered, panicked, and tearful.

There was fear on the other woman's face, and her speech was barely coherent. Miriam suspected whatever had driven Debra to Jacob, happened somewhere in the Inner City.

It took Miriam a long while to calm Debra and arrive at another option. Whoever killed Asher, and was seeking Debra, had frightened her so much, the slightest strange noise startled her.

Miriam had checked as best she could that no-one watched or followed them. She prayed she had not put Rachel and Samuel in danger.

Her own journey back into the Inner City had been swift, and with her mind on Debra and the other woman's problems, Miriam had come through the Marduk Gate with none of the fear and worry she usually felt.

Perhaps I'm getting back to normal, Miriam thought, and allowed herself a small smile.

She had sent servants to Gideon, to Jacob's house, and to Bel Ibni. Each servant carried a message asking Jacob to come to Isaac's house, as she had news for him.

Miriam glanced over the railing into the courtyard, as if just by watching the street door, she could make Jacob appear. And if she could do that, the priests of both Judah and Babylon would have her stoned and cast out as a sorceress. She gave a grim smile at the thought, returned her attention to the shawl.

Quietly, and reverently, she said the blessing prayer, and focused on the strands at the nearest corner of the shawl.

As Miriam finished the third knot, she dropped the edge of the shawl and flexed her fingers, easing away the aches in her knuckles.

Around her, the light was almost gone. She smelled the nutty scent from sesame oil lamps flickering and flaring in the courtyard below. There was the soft chatter of the servants as they prepared the evening meal. The rich aroma of onion and lentil soup fought with the scent of freshly baked barley bread.

Miriam gathered the shawl into her arms, stood, and heard her stomach growl. She was sure the noise could be heard all the way to the kitchen but, thanks be, the shrieks of laughter from Isaac's sons covered the sound of her hunger.

When Miriam arrived in the courtyard, having folded the shawl safely away, the boys had calmed. Isaac was pouring wine for himself and Jacob.

Isaac saw Miriam, poured a third goblet, and handed it to her.

"Jacob arrived moments ago. Esther will join us soon," Isaac said, then with a smile. "You'll join us for the meal, Jacob. I'm sure it will take Miriam at least that long to tell you why she sent messages all over the city of Babylon trying to find you."

"That is an offer I will gladly accept," Jacob said with a laugh. He turned to Miriam, and it seemed his voice was softer, gentler, and full of concern.

"I stopped at my house on the way to the Outer City and learned of your message. What's wrong? Are you all right?"

Miriam felt a flush of pleasure that he was worried about her.

"I'm very well," she said. She began the story about Debra, then realized the boys were watching her closely. "Perhaps my news is best left until a time when younger ears are not listening."

"An excellent decision," Esther said, joining them from the kitchen. "Jacob also looks like he has news, so you can both share after we eat."

When the meal was finished and cleared away, the boys were taken reluctantly to their beds. Isaac refilled the wine. He gestured his goblet toward Miriam, who sat beside Jacob on the long couch.

Miriam ran her fingers round the bowl of her goblet. She had spent most of the meal trying to pick the best way to tell the story, and still wasn't sure she had it right. She took a long breath and said.

"Yesterday, after we laid Asher to rest, Jacob and I saw someone watching. The person was too far away to make out anything other than a dark, hooded robe. Earlier today, when I was cleaning up, she was in the almond grove, and I spoke to her."

"You said the figure was a woman," Jacob said. "Did you learn who she is?"

"She told me her name is Debra," Miriam said, and wasn't sure whether to be amused or alarmed when Jacob nearly spilled his wine.

"Where is the poor girl?" Esther asked.

"I left her with Rachel and Samuel. She was frightened, and too scared to come into the Inner City. I couldn't think of anywhere else for her to go. She told me she spent last night in the orchard."

The nervousness and uncertainty around what she had done came back to Miriam. Her stomach fluttered, and she looked at Jacob. His brown eyes studied her with concern.

"I hope I haven't put Rachel and Samuel in danger."

"For one night, I doubt it," Jacob said.

His words, spoken firmly and without worry or concern, reassured Miriam. She felt some of the tension ease from her body.

"We should take her somewhere else, though," Jacob said. "Somewhere we can keep her out of sight, in case there are people searching for her."

"You believe that's possible?" Isaac asked.

"Likely," Jacob said. "Asher left Gideon a message scroll for me. Asher asked we find and care for Debra."

"It's fortunate she found you, Miriam," Esther said.

"I'd offer to have her here," Isaac said. "But if there's the possibility of danger, I can't risk Esther or the boys."

"I agree about Debra not staying here, Isaac, for the same reason she shouldn't be with Rachel, Samuel, and their son Enoch," Jacob said. "We don't know who she's running from, or how close to her they might be."

He sat forward, shoulders hunched, and was silent for a long while. Miriam watched as be chewed at his bottom lip, a sure sign he was thinking hard.

Finally, the tension eased from Jacob's shoulders. He took a long swallow of wine and sat back against the couch cushions.

"There's a place above the stables on the caravan grounds. It's where Bel Ibni's old caravan master, Nidintu, lived. The rooms haven't been used since Nidintu left. She can stay there. We can't send out any caravans until Arioch removes the permit ban, so there will be someone close by to protect her all the time."

And watch her, Miriam thought.

She saw Jacob glance toward her, give her the soft smile that was only for her, knew he understood her thoughts.

"When do you want to take her to the caravan grounds?" Miriam asked.

"Tomorrow," Jacob said. He looked up at the night sky. "I intended to go to the new house tonight and work on the kitchen walls in the morning before the heat becomes too much. The walls can wait another day. You and I should go to Rachel and Samuel as early as possible and take Debra to the caravan grounds."

He paused and looked across at Isaac. "With your agreement, Isaac, Solly should come with us. After we have Debra settled, I need to follow up on some of what I learned from Ligish. I'm not comfortable with Miriam returning alone."

Miriam was about to protest she had made that same journey alone earlier today, then kept her own counsel.

This was not the time for that conversation with Jacob.

Instead, she said. "Can you tell us what you learned from Ligish?"

Jacob nodded. "Of course, although it won't take long. What may take longer, and require more wine, are some thoughts I had for the house. I want your opinion on those, and any ideas you have," he said, including Esther and Isaac in the conversation.

"I'll get the wine," Isaac said.

CHAPTER NINE

The sixth day of Abu - Morning

Jacob and Miriam, with Solly in attendance, arrived at the house of Rachel and Samuel about an hour after sunrise. They were in time to share the last of the fruit and nuts Rachel had prepared for the first meal of the day.

Jacob picked at the remains of the food with little enthusiasm. He had slept poorly, tossed and turned most of the night, worrying about the problem of how to reach Nurval without spending all his time around the caravan grounds. The lack of sleep made his eyes heavy, and a slight headache nagged behind his eyes.

He knew from experience the fatigue would make his temper short, and that he needed to weigh every word before speaking.

Despite the tiredness, he couldn't resist getting down on his haunches, and spending a few moments playing with Rachel and Samuel's son, Enoch, who was nearing his fifth birthday.

After a time, Samuel reached down and plucked Enoch away from Jacob. There was surprising strength in Samuel's stick-thin arms. Enoch squealed, giggled, and kicked his feet until Samuel said some words in the boy's ear, and set him on the ground.

As Enoch scampered away, Jacob brushed the dust from his tunic, and turned to Rachel.

"Where is Debra?" he asked. "Is she still with you?"

"Of course she is," Rachel said, her dark eyes sparkling. "Did you think we'd run her off?"

"No. I..."

Rachel laughed. A rich musical sound that made Jacob smile. "She ate quickly and returned to the room we set aside for her. I don't know what she suffered. She hasn't said much, but she is terrified."

"Miriam warned me," Jacob said. "Perhaps one or both of you should see her first and prepare her for meeting me."

"I'll make sure Samuel and I stay out of your way," Rachel said.

Jacob saw something in her dark eyes then. Understanding, or a realization perhaps, of what she had agreed to the previous evening. In a lower voice pitched so only Jacob could hear, Rachel said. "Are we in danger? Samuel, Enoch, and I?"

Jacob shook his head. "I'm sure you're safe, but to be certain, I am taking Debra to another place in case someone is looking for her. We'll talk with her as we travel."

"Thank you," Rachel said, then reached out for Miriam's arm. "Come and help me find Debra a comb, some bands for her hair, and other things she may need."

Miriam gave him a quick smile as she let herself be pulled away. Jacob watched as the two women disappeared inside the house and said a prayer, asking that he hadn't given Rachel false reassurances.

They reappeared several minutes later, a young woman between, and almost a half-pace behind them.

"This is Debra," Miriam said as the trio stopped several paces from him.

She wasn't at all what Jacob expected. Debra was maybe twenty summers and much younger than Asher. If Jacob had chosen for his friend, it would have been a strong woman. A woman who would stand toe-to-toe with him during his moods, and battle beside him in times of adversity.

Debra looked like a sudden wind, or harsh word, would topple her over.

Her black hair hung in a twisted tangle around her high cheekbones. The marks under her dark eyes were nearly as black as her hair.

Jacob guessed she had slept as badly as he had, and he hadn't slept in an orchard the night before that.

There was a child's wail from inside the house. Rachel rolled her eyes, gave an apologetic shrug, and hurried away.

"I wish we had met under happier circumstances, Debra," Jacob said. "I am Jacob. You told Miriam you were looking for me. What can we do for you?"

"I'm not sure," Debra said, her head down, hands clasped together, long slender fingers kneading each other. "Asher said I was to find you if anything happened to him, but he never said about after that, and I never thought to ask."

She spoke excellent Aramaic, although with an accent Jacob didn't recognize. It wasn't from Judah, or his own land, the land of the Benjaminites.

"How long have you been in Babylon?"

She looked surprised at his question. "All my life. My father's family were carpenters, taken from Samaria many years ago."

The Assyrians, Jacob guessed. They conquered the northern kingdom of Israel over a hundred years before and, like the Babylonians, had forcibly deported thousands of people.

And Debra, like Enoch, would likely never know her homeland, or experience the joy of prayer in the Temple in Jerusalem.

"Is your family safe?" Miriam asked.

Debra shook her head. "There's only me now. My father died soon after I was born. My mother passed three moons ago."

Jacob felt a surge of relief, then a pang of guilt. It would be hard enough to protect Debra. Much harder if she had other family members as well. At least he was spared that burden.

Debra's next words broke into his thoughts.

"Your friends, Samuel and Rachel. Did they know Asher?"

"No," Miriam said before Jacob could answer.

"I have known Rachel since we were children. She and her husband allowed you to stay here as a favor to me."

"I never had the chance to meet any of Asher's friends," Debra said. "I wanted to learn so much more about him."

She turned away then, covering her face with the sleeve of her robe, but not before Jacob saw the glitter of tears in her eyes.

He smiled at Miriam, letting her know he understood what she had done, and that he agreed with it. Her smile in response was strained.

"Debra," he said, and waited until she wiped her face and looked at him. "When this matter is done, I will be happy to sit with you and tell you many stories. So will the others who knew him. For now, though, we must leave Miriam's friends and take you to a place where you can be properly protected. On the way, I have some questions for you."

"For me?"

"I need to know when and where you were last with Asher, Debra. I need to find out if you know where he was going, and what made you come looking for me."

She looked scared suddenly. Her eyes went wide and her hands trembled.

Jacob spoke quickly. "Not here. I understand you're frightened about people hearing and putting you in danger again. We'll talk of this as we walk, and you can speak freely before Miriam. I trust her completely."

"I know," Debra said. She gave Miriam a tentative smile. "If it wasn't for Miriam, I'd still be in the orchard, or somewhere worse."

Debra ran her hands through her hair, trying to comb her tangled tresses into a semblance of order. She turned her head around like she was looking for Rachel or Samuel.

"I wanted to thank your friends, but maybe another time." She shrugged. "I'm ready whenever you are."

"We'll leave now. Miriam can give her apologies another time," Jacob said.

He ushered the two women before him, with Solly a few paces behind. When they reached the road and turned left toward the Outer Ramparts and the caravan grounds, Jacob made certain they were both on his right-hand side. It left his sword arm free in case they were attacked. He didn't think it was likely, but until he knew more about how Debra came to them, he wasn't taking any chances.

There were few people on the dusty road that ran beside the irrigation canal in a north-south direction. Jacob waited until a group of four women passed them, then said.

"Debra. You told us Asher wanted you to find me. What made you come now?"

He counted twenty paces before she answered.

"We had a room at a small inn in Kweiresh, right over the room where the innkeeper brewed his beer. The smell was awful, and seemed to be all around the inn, and even got into our clothes," she said, wrinkling her nose at the memory.

"We were there for four or five days when Asher left to meet someone. I don't know who, as he never told me. He didn't come back, and two evenings ago, two men came to the inn asking for him. They scared me, and I fled to look for you."

"I think that's near a woman who finds some of my herbs, and yes, that beer smell is terrible," Miriam said. She shared a smile with Debra. "Do you remember what the two men looked like?"

"Not really. It was evening and nearly dark. They were bigger than me, and talked with a strange accent, like Akkadian was a new language for them. There was a way out into an alley behind the inn. Asher told me you were building a house between the Inner Wall and Outer Ramparts, close to the road that goes over the Nil Bridge, so that's where I looked."

Jacob said nothing as they passed another group of travelers, heard them exchange greetings with Solly. It was barely mid-morning, but the heat was as intense as the middle of the day, making it hard to concentrate and to order the dates and events in his mind.

When he last saw Asher, had he told him about the house, or mentioned he was still considering the property?

Jacob couldn't recall. He knew it was something to return to when the air was cooler and he had slept better.

"How did you meet Asher?" he asked.

"In the strangest of ways," Debra said. "I was delivering fabrics to a house in Borsippa. It was work my mother finished before she died. Asher was at the house and it was late when I finished. He escorted me back to Babylon, and we became close."

She half-turned and gestured to Solly, still trailing behind them. "I never had a chaperone like you have. I hope you're not shocked or offended. Once Asher decided I was for him, it didn't matter."

"Asher was like that," Jacob said. "Very single minded once he made a decision. It got him in trouble more than once."

"And you, I suspect," Miriam said.

"And me," Jacob said, making them both laugh.

It pleased Jacob that Miriam spoke up. She had been quiet for much of the journey, like there was something on her mind. He hoped she wasn't worried about Rachel and Samuel's safety

Jacob decided he would talk with Gideon and arrange for someone to watch their house.

Just in case.

Ahead of them, the road curved away to the northeast toward the outer gates and the road to Sippar. On their left, shrouded in a haze of dust, was the sprawling collection of stables, storehouses, and sleeping quarters, all built with mud-bricks and roofed with more brick or reed thatch.

This was the place where the merchants assembled the caravans that traded all across the Babylonian empire. Beyond the staging area were the sheep and goat pens for the temple herds.

As they left the road and began the journey toward the staging area assigned to Jacob and Bel Ibni, Jacob noted the increasing hesitation in Debra's step, sensed the fear that came off her tense body.

"Is something wrong?" Jacob asked.

"Where are you taking me?" Debra answered with a question of her own.

"Somewhere safe," Jacob said

He saw the fearful shake of her head, realized that wasn't the real question she had asked.

"There's a place you can stay where we assemble our caravans. We are a long way from the road. I doubt anyone will think to look for you there, but you'll have people around you all the time."

Debra relaxed a little then, the tension easing from her face.

"Thank you," she said, and lengthened her stride to keep up.

As the four of them reached the edge of the area assigned to Bel

Ibni, Jacob saw a group of men break up, most of them walking toward the stables, laughing and joking amongst themselves.

A single man watched them approach.

Jacob recognized the lone man as Sibri, a man who had worked for Bel Ibni for many years. Now, after an accident, when a mule rolled onto his leg, Sibri mostly managed the mules they used for their caravans.

Sibri looked at Jacob, then Miriam, and finally at Debra. There was a teasing smile on his sharp, angular face. "Are you collecting a pack of wives, Jacob? I thought your people had abandoned that practice."

Jacob heard the chuckle of amusement from Miriam, sensed again the sudden tension in Debra's body.

"Once again, Sibri, you speak before your mind thinks," he said. "Debra came to us for help. I need her somewhere safe where no-one will talk."

The smile remained on Sibri's face. Since the recent expedition to Nineveh, where Sibri had proven he could still lead a caravan, Jacob suspected very little would remove it.

"You're thinking of the rooms Nidintu used?" Sibri asked.

"I am."

Sibri rubbed his hand across his beard, scratched at the side of his nose. "It's still as Nidintu left it. Which means it's a mess. I'll get some men to clean it out and bring in fresh straw and blankets. It will take a while, but we have fresh bread, a barley soup, and beer if you want to eat while you wait."

"That will be good," Jacob said. "Let's get Miriam and Debra to the food, then you and I can talk about what she needs."

"What she needs, or what you want for her?"

"It's the same," Jacob said. "I want her kept here and safe, Sibri. Her life may be in danger."

CHAPTER TEN

The sixth day of Abu - Afternoon

Miriam was glad to be away from the caravan grounds. It always smelled of mules, mule droppings, and straw used too many times. It was a smell that churned her stomach and tainted the food Sibri provided for them.

The constant movement of men and animals left a fine haze of dust over her clothes, skin, and in her hair. The dust drifted into her nose, making her feel like she was about to sneeze at any time.

And no matter how hard Sibri tried to prevent it, the dust got into the food and the beer. Her mouth felt like she had a film of sand in it. She hoped they found a better way to serve the food, so Debra didn't have grit in everything she ate or drank.

They had left Jacob giving instructions to Sibri. When Miriam reached the road, she paused. She had set a fast pace between the many stables and sleeping quarters. Solly was twenty or thirty paces behind her, his face red from the exertion, his breath coming in wheezing gasps.

"Rest here, Solly," she said, as he reached her.

"I don't like the place much either," Solly said, when his breathing was back to normal.

His head was still down, looking at a pile of mud-bricks on the side of the road. Miriam didn't think he really saw the bricks.

"All the dust and noise, and the smell of the animals," Solly said in a voice that was little more than a whisper. "It reminds me too much of the trek from Jerusalem."

"You should have told me. You could have stayed with Isaac," Miriam said, wondering if he was well enough for her to follow the plan she had come up with during the conversation with Debra on the way to the caravan grounds.

"Can you manage a visit to Kweiresh, or would you rather return to Isaac's home?"

Solly's head came up then. There was a sparkle in his dark eyes, a half-smile on his lined face. "All I do at Isaac's is sit and wait for someone to come to the house. With you, at least I'm being useful. I suspect your Jacob doesn't know about this trip to Kweiresh."

"He doesn't," Miriam said. "I want to talk to Ruth, the woman I buy herbs from in Kweiresh. It's probably nothing, and will be a waste of our time, but I want to be sure."

"Do you have your needle?" Solly asked.

Miriam nodded.

She had the bone needle tucked into a strip of linen wound around her left forearm under the sleeve of her robe. She started carrying the needle after being kidnapped at the Marduk Gate. The needle had saved her life, and that of another man. Now she wore it whenever she left the Inner City.

Solly smiled again, revealing stained and crooked teeth. He patted the sword strapped to his belt. "I think we'll be all right."

Miriam smiled back.

Instead of heading south toward the Marduk Gate, they followed a narrower path that followed the irrigation canal north-west toward the Euphrates river, and the village of Kweiresh.

The sun was getting lower in the western sky when they reached Kweiresh. The smell of burning and smoke from the furnaces got stronger as they entered the village. Miriam had her hand over her forehead to shield her eyes from the glare, but she still had to keep her eyes half-closed to see anything. The shade and shadow of the first buildings was a relief, and she was glad to rest both her eyes and her legs.

Beside her, Solly leaned against the rough mud-brick wall, his face flushed and covered in sweat. "We should have brought water with us," he said with a croak.

"We should have," Miriam said. "It's not much farther, Solly. Just a few streets. We'll find something to drink when we arrive, and not the beer from the inn."

Solly followed faithfully as Miriam led him through the side streets of Kweiresh. Two streets from their destination, Miriam could smell the beer being brewed. She thought it smelled worse than usual, but perhaps it was the heat adding its own ingredient. The smell grew stronger, and less pleasant, with every step until they reached the house where Miriam bought most of the fresh herbs she couldn't grow herself.

Like many of the small stores in Babylon and the surrounding villages, the shop was on the bottom floor of the house. Miriam and Solly pushed through the hanging ox-hide into a room about ten paces square. Rows of fresh herbs hung from hooks on the walls, with lighting provided by sesame oil lamps. An iron brazier, hip high, the coals still warm, nestled in a corner. A heavy gray blanket hung across a doorway on the far side of the room. The fragrance of the herbs, and the nutty smell of the sesame oil, almost destroyed the brewing beer smell that was so heavy outside.

"Give me a moment," a woman's voice sounded from an upper level of the house. "I'll be with you as soon as I can."

While they waited, Miriam walked along the rows of herbs, bringing some to her nose to test the freshness, gently rubbing others between her thumb and forefinger to release the scent.

There was a clatter of feet on a staircase. The blanket billowed and moved aside. A red-faced woman, at least a head shorter than Miriam, and twice as wide, came into the room. Her right hand was behind her back, and there was something in her dark eyes that conflicted with the look of welcome on her ruddy face.

"I hope we aren't disturbing you, Ruth." Miriam said, moving toward the woman. Ruth hesitated, then did something with her right hand, brought it in front of her body, and embraced Miriam.

"Hardly."

Ruth waved her arm to take in the room. "I'm not exactly busy today. You're looking well, Miriam. I wasn't expecting you for another seven or eight days. Did you use all those herbs already?"

"Most of them," Miriam said. "I really need more rosemary if you have any."

The woman tilted her head to one side. Her lips moved silently for a moment, and then she nodded. "I have plenty of rosemary, and some of the tarkhun you were asking about last time."

"I'll take the rosemary, and four bunches of the tarkhun if you have that much," Miriam said, pleased her diversion had provided an unexpected bonus.

She waited until the woman handed over the herbs wrapped in a piece of damp cloth to keep them fresh, the spicy licorice smell of the tarkhun tickling her nose.

"I heard you had some excitement at the inn a night or so ago," Miriam said.

The look was back in Ruth's eyes, Miriam thought as the other woman shook her head, made a dismissive noise in her throat.

"There's always excitement of some sort over there. I know the men need to drink, and some need a place to stay for the night, but I'd appreciate if they made less noise."

She peered at the copper coins Miriam handed over, moved her hand, and they disappeared. Miriam assumed the coins went into a pocket of the woman's robe, but she was never sure.

"A few nights ago?" Ruth said. "I don't know that you'd call it excitement, not for the couple involved."

"What happened?"

Ruth folded her arms across her chest, rested her bottom on the table behind her, and took a long breath that told Miriam this would be a long story.

"They've never been concerned about the type of people they serve there. Or worried about the smell of their brewing. I wouldn't mind so much if the beer was at least drinkable, but I wouldn't force that brew on my worst enemy."

Ruth paused, tilted her head to one side, then back again, and let a smile twist her face. "Well, maybe there's one or two."

"It was late," she continued. "Well past the time I normally get noise. There was a crashing and banging and shouting. I heard a woman scream and looked out from my room up on the floor above. There were four men in the alley below. Three of them were dragging another man away. The fourth tried to take the woman. She wasn't having any of it, and good for her. I didn't see what she did to him, but he squealed like a goat does just before you give it that final blow."

"What happened to the woman?" Miriam asked.

"No idea. She ran off down the alley in the opposite direction, her long hair trailing behind her like sand off the dunes after that storm near Rabat Aman. You remember that storm, Miriam? It was just after your husband, Nahum, disappeared."

"I remember the storm," Miriam said.

She couldn't imagine Debra's shoulder length hair flying the way Ruth described. Miriam remembered the storm Ruth spoke of, and the relief she felt as well.

The relief coming from the knowledge Nahum had almost certainly died in the storm, and whatever the hardships she had before her, she was free of him.

Miriam took a long breath. She didn't need those memories now.

"I heard the woman might need help. Do you know where she went?"

"Back to Judah, if she has any sense," Ruth said with a harsh cackle, then became serious, shook her head. "She isn't around here, I'd have heard. It's unlikely, but you might find something in the room they rented."

"It hasn't been cleaned out, or given to someone else?"

Another cackle, and Ruth shook her head again. "The man paid for two months, and there's no-one looking to rent a room in a place like Simon's unless they have no other options. I wouldn't go inside if you paid me. I doubt Simon's done more than put the door back, if that much. Give him some coppers and he'll let you clean the room yourself."

It took four pieces of copper, and an uncharacteristically aggressive snarl from Solly, before Simon, the innkeeper, let Miriam through to the rented sleeping rooms.

The room Miriam wanted was on the left side at the end of a narrow hallway. As Ruth predicted, the door was splintered and broken, and propped against the wall.

At the far end of the hallway, an outside doorway, partially covered with a strip of cloth, let heat in from the alleyway. The sour smell of urine and other human waste drifted in and hung heavy in the air.

Solly coughed. Miriam covered her face with the sleeve of her robe.

"Stay here," Miriam said to Solly.

She walked past the room to the outside doorway, pushed the strip of ragged, stained cloth aside so she could see into the alleyway.

To her right, the alley ran in a straight line past Ruth's house and on to the Main Street. On the left, a dozen paces away, was the high mud-brick wall of another building.

Miriam studied the scene for a moment. She held her breath against the foul smell.

Something tickled in her mind.

Something that told her something was wrong. She stood there, shielding her eyes against the sun's glare until it became necessary to breathe.

Miriam released the breath she'd been holding. She turned back toward the room they had come to search, still with a feeling of something amiss.

The room was about five paces by four, with a ripped and stained straw mattress on the floor. A cracked chamber pot lay on its side against the far wall, the spilled contents a dried and crusty stain on the floor that mingled with the sour odor from the outside.

For a moment, Miriam feared she was going to empty her stomach onto the mess on the floor.

She shook her head, scolded herself. She had seen worse on the trek into Exile. Worse when she was kidnapped.

Miriam took a deep breath, held it, and stepped all the way into the room.

She stayed close to the wall, let her eyes become accustomed to the half-light in the room. There was a blanket across the window set high on the wall opposite the doorway. Miriam reached out, pulled the blanket free so a band of bright light carved a rectangle across the room. It didn't make that much difference to the overall light, but allowed Miriam to identify specific items.

There was a dark brown robe in one corner, balled up and discarded like it was no longer needed. Beside the robe was a bundle of linens that looked like a woman's undergarments.

Miriam reached her foot out, nudged the clothing with the clothing with the edge of her sandal, heard something chink onto the floor.

"Are you all right, Miriam?" Solly poked his head round the side of the doorway, one hand over his mouth and nose.

"I'm fine," she said, poked again at the clothing with her foot until a metallic shape revealed itself on the floor. She lifted the hem of her robe, stepped over a puddle of something dark and congealed, and picked up the piece of metal.

It was surprisingly cold in her hands, and more than simple metal.

Miriam could tell from the weight and the feel of it in her hands, the cloak clasp she held was solid silver.

She moved back to the doorway, used the sunlight coming through the window to better see what she had. Miriam turned the silver clasp over in her hand and studied it.

"What did you find?" Solly asked

"A silver cloak clasp," Miriam said. She turned the clasp toward the window, letting the light catch on the clasp so the brighter light high-lighted the design.

Miriam felt her breath catch.

A menorah. She leaned forward, studied the markings and the shape of the design. It was a design she recognized. The clasp came from the Temple in Jerusalem, the work of Eli the silversmith.

She was sure, certain, when she turned the clasp over, saw the tiny mark Eli always added to identify his work.

Nahum had given her a clasp almost identical just after they married. The only present he ever gave her, other than his death.

Solly leaned forward, his hand closing over hers as he tilted the clasp, so he could see it for himself.

"This is Eli's work," he said. "How is it here?"

Miriam had wondered that herself. Then a simple solution came to her. "Most likely Asher gave it to Debra."

"Then he's cleverer than many of us. Isaac included," Solly said, releasing his hold on the clasp. "That piece has real value. Isaac couldn't get more than a dozen silver coins past the Babylonian soldiers."

He looked past Miriam, his eyes taking in the mess in the room. "There's more happened in this room than that girl told you."

CHAPTER ELEVEN

The sixth day of Abu - Afternoon

Jacob placed the last brick in the row that marked the kitchen wall, nudged it into place, then adjusted it so the base lined up with the row below.

He stepped back, wiped the sweat from his brow, and sighted along the wall, making sure that like the last brick, each of its predecessors aligned with the row below and there were no bulges or indentations that could weaken the finished structure.

Jacob had begun the work as soon as he reached the house after leaving the caravan grounds with Debra hidden safely with Sibri.

This was the fourth course of bricks he'd laid. Now, with the sun beginning to sink lower in the sky, it was time to finish this work for the day. The next courses of bricks required him to build a simple scaffold, and that was best done in the cooler air of the morning.

And his right arm was sore. Really sore. The muscles that had never fully healed after the sword strike ached and complained at any prolonged use, and Jacob had worked them hard today.

Jacob promised himself he would devote the next day to searching for Asher's killers. The construction work had helped clear his head and think about the problem of Asher's killers with less emotion than he felt the previous day. He wasn't sure the three men he'd discussed with Ligish and Bel Ibni the previous day were those he searched for, but he had to begin somewhere.

He wiped his hands clean, collected a bag and water skin, and walked down through the almond orchard, studying the fruit hanging from the branches as he did so. Jacob learned more about the trees every day, guessed he had another moon, maybe two, before the almonds would be ready to harvest. With luck, the house would be finished by then.

With even more luck, the Judah caravan would have returned, and he would be married to Miriam.

At the lower edge of the orchard, Jacob sat in a patch of shade beside Asher's grave. He took a large mouthful of water from the waterskin, picked dates and nuts from the bag, chewed on them as he gazed east without really seeing the landscape. His thoughts drifted immediately to Miriam, but he forced his mind away from her and toward Iddin.

Whatever his attempts at reform, Jacob remained convinced that at heart, Iddin remained committed to the evil he visited on the unsuspecting and unfortunate among the residents and visitors of Babylon.

Iddin was a natural suspect. And perhaps too convenient, Jacob thought. He still could not see the gain for Iddin if the man controlled Arioch, or Arioch's replacement.

The rustle of leaves and crackle twigs being broken brought Jacob back to the present. He looked to his left, toward the noise, saw a shadow, then recognized the figure coming toward him.

Jacob stood and brushed crumbs from this tunic as the priest reached him. The man was stick thin. Wisps of gray hair came off his head at all angles, shining silver in the bright sun, and making his dark eyes seem even darker.

When Jacob first met the man on the steps of the Temple in Jerusalem, he looked so frail that Jacob expected the slightest puff of breeze to knock him down.

Jacob knew better now.

The man came forward, not pausing until he reached Jacob, and then he folded his arms around Jacob.

"Gideon told me about Asher. I'm sorry."

Jacob hugged the man back. "Thank you, Ezra. There was no need for you to come."

Ezra stepped back. He huffed a snort, and his dark eyes twinkled. "I'm a priest, Jacob. Someone needed to come and make sure you followed some sort of tradition when you laid Asher to rest."

"I had Isaac and Samuel. And Miriam," Jacob said, unable to keep the smile from his face.

"Miriam's presence calms my fears," Ezra said with a smile of his own.

"I have wine and some simple food at the house," Jacob said. "We can talk there."

They sat cross-legged on the dusty earth with their backs leaning against the kitchen wall Jacob had worked on earlier that day. The recent work gave them shade from the bright sunlight. Jacob laid out the fruit and nuts, passed the wineskin to Ezra.

"How are you here without an escort of junior priests and acolytes?"

Ezra took a long swallow from the wineskin, passed it back to Jacob. "You know the house of the priests in the Ka-Dingirra district of the Inner City?"

"I've been there," Jacob said.

"I have a room there where I pray and meditate alone and in silence. Everyone, and I mean everyone, knows not to disturb me, even if I am there for a full day or longer. There is a way out of the house and into the alley behind it. From there, I can see what is actually happening to our people without formal visits or the truth shading many of my colleagues prefer."

"I appreciate you paying your respects to Asher. He would have liked that."

"I'm sure he'd prefer to be here sharing this wineskin," Ezra said. "Gideon also told me a little of what Asher was doing for the people in the Esagila. There are things you should know."

The tone in the words made Jacob put the wineskin aside. He held the other man's gaze. "You didn't approve?"

Ezra picked up the wineskin, wiped a layer of dust off the spout, and took another long swallow. "I assume this is the wine from Nineveh. It's very good, and I'm most disappointed you sell so much of it to the Babylonians and save none for your own priests."

"I have some casks I can send you," Jacob said. "For you only, though, and be frugal with them. I don't know when we might get more. And you didn't answer my question."

"I took your words to be a statement," Ezra said. "Actually, I did approve. Like you, I can work with Arioch. Despite how some of our other priests feel, I have no desire to see Arioch removed. The alternatives would not be good for our people."

"Subisha?"

Ezra shook his head. "I understand why Arioch suspects him, but I believe he's wrong. Have you met Subisha?"

Jacob brushed some dust off a date, popped it into his mouth, let the sweet juices roll over his tongue before he answered. "I've seen him from a distance. Everything I know about him comes from Ligish and Bel Ibni."

"You should try to meet him," Ezra said. "He gives me the feeling he is not of this world. I had the same sense whenever I met Jeremiah, before Jerusalem fell, and he fled to Egypt. Subisha is lucky that he has two assistants who know more about the Esagila and its ways than he does."

"Comparing Subisha to one of our prophets is praise indeed," Jacob said, reaching for the wineskin. "Are there other things I can learn from you?"

"Gideon told me Nurval is hard to reach. It is possible I can help there."

Jacob felt his heart quicken. He had worried about that problem most of the night. "How?"

"Nurval's wife insists on staying at the palace with her family whenever they come to Babylon. I've seen both of them often. Nurval is at the palace when he's not on the caravan grounds."

"I had thought of waiting for Nurval on the caravan grounds. I went past there earlier today. He has enough guards around that area to make waiting a dangerous idea."

"Nurval is a very cautious man," Ezra said. "He leaves the palace before the curfew ends and returns late in the morning. The rest of the day he spends with his family."

"Can you help me get into the palace so I can talk to him there?"

"I could," Ezra said. "However, there are too many of our people in the palace who will recognize you, and that may not be for the best."

Jacob nodded.

In the last days of the siege of Jerusalem, and during the journey into Exile, Jacob had unwittingly made enemies of several influential members of the Judean King's court, and some priests. Those still alive had long memories. And some who had never known him in Jerusalem also considered him their enemy.

"I understand," he said, barely able to keep the disappointment from his voice.

Ezra smiled like he had just won everything in a game of chance. "By coincidence, three days ago, Priest Noah and his associates left Babylon to visit the Judean community in Erech. A young woman in the Queen's entourage is having trouble with her pregnancy. She is not comfortable with the midwives attending her, and it would be appropriate for Miriam to visit."

"No!"

The word was out before Jacob had time to even considered his response.

"I think yes," Ezra said with a soft smile.

"I know you want to protect her, Jacob, but Miriam has proven more than once she can take excellent care of herself. She will be under my protection in the palace, and always in sight of myself or one of the few other men I trust completely."

Jacob still wanted to say no, but the more he considered the idea, the less opposition he had to it. He took a long swallow from the wineskin.

"Only if Miriam agrees," he said.

Ezra took the wineskin, his face a huge grin. "In what world do you imagine she will say no?"

CHAPTER TWELVE

The sixth day of Abu - Evening

When Miriam and Solly arrived back at Isaac's house, the sun was below the western walls of Babylon. The shade in the streets was a welcome relief from the sun's glare, and it seemed the heat was less intense despite how close the houses were to each other.

As they came through the doorway into the house, the sound of chatter and laughter flooded over them. Miriam exchanged a confused glance with Solly, who shrugged his shoulders.

The servants hustled back and forth, setting the table with everything required for a full feast. Esther's sons, in good clothes, weaved and dodged between the servants and their father as he stood talking with two men.

Miriam recognized one of the men.

How could she not? She thought. Even with his back to her, Miriam knew it was Jacob. She was pleased he was here to share their meal, felt her heart beat a little faster.

The other man, also with his back toward her, and thin as a walking staff, Miriam felt she should recognize. For the moment, she couldn't place him.

"There you are."

Esther appeared at Miriam's side. Her face was flushed, beads of perspiration trickled down the side of her face onto her ample cheeks.

"Are we having a celebration? What's the occasion?" Miriam asked.

"Jacob is here with a priest and. . ."

Miriam missed the rest of Esther's words. The blood pounded in her ears. Her stomach clenched. Her throat constricted.

Priest.

Noah!

Why couldn't the man leave her alone? Why couldn't he leave all of them alone?

"Miriam!"

The sharpness of Esther's tone brought Miriam back to the present.

"I'm sorry, Esther," she said. "You surprised me."

"I doubt news of Jacob being here surprised you," Esther said, her voice softer. "And why Ezra's name makes you look like a frightened deer, I do not know."

"I didn't hear you say Ezra's name. I just heard priest."

Understanding flooded across Esther's face. The last of the harshness faded from her face, but remained in her tone. "That other one would not have passed through the door. I've made that very clear to Isaac, and he agrees with me." Esther looked down at the package in Miriam's hand, then glanced up at the darkening sky.

"Hurry and put those herbs somewhere they'll keep. It's a rare occasion we have the chance to celebrate evening prayer with a real priest, and you won't want to miss it."

"I'll have a servant take the herbs, then I'll be ready," Miriam said.

She had celebrated both morning and evening prayer many, many times with real priests, as Esther described them. Her father, then her husband, and other priests from the Temple in Jerusalem. Miriam preferred simple prayers with family and friends. Those prayers felt more honest and relevant to her life than all the elaborate words and phrases chanted by the priests.

Small wonder her father had despaired of her.

As Miriam took her place beside Jacob, he turned, looked down at her, a question in his rich brown eyes.

"Later," she said. "There's much to tell."

He opened his mouth to reply.

Ezra's voice spoke as he started the first prayer, his voice deep and rich, resonating around the courtyard like the tones after a bell is struck.

Jacob closed his mouth and nodded.

Miriam felt a shiver of gratitude ripple through her as Ezra chanted the last words of the last prayer.

Sometimes, she admitted to herself, a real priest made all the difference to worship.

She had felt the difference inside her the moment Ezra began the first prayer. The sense of joy and wonder, and being as one with Yahweh. It had been so long since she felt that connection, and there were tears in her eyes as she repeated the last response.

Ezra lowered his arms.

The moment lingered.

Miriam used the pad of her forefinger to wipe her eyes, saw Jacob watching her.

"If every priest was like Ezra," Jacob said in a low voice. "The Temple would still stand in Jerusalem, and the Babylonians would be our subjects."

"And you would be a soldier, and I the wife of a priest," she said. "It has been hard, but I think I prefer this to what you suggested."

"The correct answer, Jacob, is to acknowledge how right Miriam is," Ezra said, coming to stand beside them. He patted his hand ineffectively at the unruly wisps of gray hair on his head, trying to bring them into some sort of order.

"As a former soldier, I was thinking of a retreat to the jug of fine wine Isaac has just placed on the table."

"Also acceptable," Ezra said. "As long as you pour for Miriam and myself as well."

Miriam joined Jacob in the laughter and followed him to the table.

"How did you get Ezra away from the other priests and bring him here?" she asked as he handed her a goblet of wine.

"He found me," Jacob said. He told her about Ezra coming to the house and saying a blessing over Asher's grave.

"There's much more to tell," he said as Isaac called them to the meal. "We'll share our stories after we've eaten."

With so little time to prepare, Miriam was amazed at the meal Esther had brought together. The only meat was strips of roasted goat rubbed with more spices than Miriam could identify, some of them so hot they almost burned her mouth. She was grateful for the mild soothing sauces, and the barley stew that took the edge off the heat and allowed the flavor of the milder spices to come through.

The conversation stayed light throughout the meal, and ranged over several topics, but never touched on the reason for Ezra's attendance. Jacob looked distracted, eating without really tasting the food, using his fingers to move the wine goblet in small circles without taking more than a sip at a time.

Miriam sympathized with his struggle not to move the conversation to the events of the day. She had the same challenge herself and concentrated hard to keep her attention on Esther and Isaac as they talked with Ezra about schooling for their sons.

Finally, the servants cleared the table, and Esther took the boys away. Isaac had the servants bring more wine. When dishes of dates and nuts were placed, and goblets refilled, Isaac pushed to his feet.

"My curiosity wants me to stay and hear what you have learned, and what you plan to do next," he said. "My sense of self-preservation takes me inside so you can speak freely."

Both Ezra and Jacob tried to talk Isaac into staying, but he was adamant about his decision.

"I feel like I've made Isaac unwelcome in his own home," Ezra said, once they were alone.

"Some things it's better he doesn't hear," Jacob said.

His words confirmed Miriam's suspicion Ezra and Jacob were also glad Isaac had left them. Then Jacob looked at Miriam.

"Tell us about your afternoon first," he said.

Miriam had spent most of the meal preparing herself, but still took a small sip of wine before speaking.

"You recall when Debra mentioned the smell of the brewing in

Kweiresh? I get some of my herbs from a woman who has a similar unpleasant smell close to her home. Solly and I visited the woman."

"A good idea," Jacob said. "What happened?"

Miriam took another sip of wine and told them the rest of the story. She didn't tell them about the look in Ruth's eyes.

"You're sure about the clasp?" Ezra asked when she finished.

"Certain."

Miriam reached into the pocket of her robe, pulled out the clasp, and offered it to Ezra.

Ezra leaned forward, studied the clasp in the flickering light of the lamp on the table, then passed it to Jacob.

She watched Jacob hold the clasp in his palm and judge the weight before angling it toward the lamp. The light made the polished silver sparkle and shine. It highlighted the delicate lines of the menorah and the squiggle of Eli's mark.

"Could Eli have made this in Babylon after the Exile?" Jacob asked.

Ezra shook his head. "No. He was already old when Jerusalem fell, and the journey into Exile wasn't kind to him. His hands are like claws now, and this sort of fine work is impossible for him."

"What about someone copying his work?"

"I know Eli's work," Miriam said, ignoring the look Jacob sent her way. She'd tell him later. "This is one of Eli's creations. My question is, how did Debra have it if her family was taken during the Assyrian deportations?"

"A gift from Asher?" Ezra suggested.

"No," Jacob said, handing the clasp back to Miriam. "I have little experience of jewelry like this, but I know the cost is beyond anything Asher could afford. We had nothing of value when we left Jerusalem, and the Babylonian army pays no better than the Judean one."

"We could ask Debra," Miriam said, and felt no surprise when Jacob shook his head emphatically.

"Let's keep this amongst the three of us for now," he said, then smiled at Miriam as he reached for the dates. "I suppose it's time to tell you about our afternoon."

She laughed at Ezra's reason for visiting Jacob and blushed at the confidence Ezra had in her handling of Asher's burial.

"The longer we are here, the more our people put tradition aside. I'm grateful you keep to our traditions the best you can," Ezra said, then shrugged and offered Miriam an apologetic smile. "Now, we break with tradition and ask you to do something Jacob is not happy about."

Miriam sat straighter, tried to catch Jacob's eye. He wouldn't meet her look, kept his gaze on a guttering lamp on the far side of the courtyard.

"Nurval is a hard man to reach," Jacob said in a low voice. "I am going to try at the caravan grounds in the morning, but likely I'll be unsuccessful. Ezra can get you into the palace where he's staying with his wife. We are hoping you can get a message to him."

Jacob looked at her then, and she saw the pain and worry in his brown eyes. "I can't be with you. Too many of the Judean nobles know me and have no love for me."

Miriam understood what he left unsaid. Some nobles and priests had long, bitter memories, and would welcome the chance to finish something started in the last days of the siege of Jerusalem. It was a story she had never heard in full. She vowed to herself that one day soon, she would ask Jacob to tell her everything.

Now was not the time, though. Perhaps when she told him how she knew about Eli's work.

Another thought came to her. "I'm also well known among our priests, Ezra. I don't want any chance of seeing Noah."

"On that subject, we are blessed," Ezra said with an understanding nod of his head. "Jacob had similar fears, and I have assured him there will be no problems. Noah and those who follow him left for Erech three days ago."

Miriam felt the relief wash over her. She looked at Ezra, then at Jacob. "With the condition that Esther comes with me, I'll do it," she said.

CHAPTER THIRTEEN

The seventh day of Abu - Late Morning

There seemed to be more rubbish and refuse in the street when Jacob reached Gideon's inn late the next morning. The summer heat was as intense and uncomfortable as it had been for the past few days, and the smell from the refuse seemed fouler and more intense.

Jacob held his breath as he reached the open doorway. He ducked his head, went down the step to the inside, and shivered a little in the sudden transition from heat to the relative coolness inside the inn.

A group of men sat round a table with jugs of beer between them. They talked in low tones, and Jacob wondered if it was the same group of laborers he had seen three days before.

He scanned the rest of the room, squinting his eyes, trying to see better in the dim light. He jumped when a hand touched his arm.

"Your friend is waiting in the third booth," the serving girl said. She gestured toward a booth with the curtain pulled across it. Today, she had her ebony hair pulled back and tied into a ponytail, revealing her thin, pale face.

"Does he have beer yet?"

She nodded. "And a spare tankard."

Jacob thanked her, handed her a copper coin, crossed the room and slipped behind the heavy fabric.

Ligish looked up as Jacob slid into the seat. He reached over and poured beer into the empty tankard in front of Jacob. "This is Gideon's latest attempt at a Judean beer," he said. "I'll let you decide, but it doesn't taste like the beers I drank in Jerusalem."

"They probably served you the moldy beer in Jerusalem," Jacob said with a smile, and lifted the tankard to his mouth.

Ligish returned the smile. "I suspected as much. What do you think of this beer?"

Jacob took another sip, said. "Better than the last attempt, but still too sour." He held the tankard beside the sesame oil lamp, tilted the tankard slightly, and studied the contents. "Not dark enough either."

"I'm not qualified to comment on the color, but I agree about the taste. Gideon says he has another batch coming that's much better," Ligish said. "Have you learned anything in the last two days?"

"Not much," Jacob said.

Quickly, he brought Ligish up to date.

"Finding Debra is more than not much," Ligish said. "I wouldn't have thought to approach Nurval in the Summer palace either." He gave a short laugh. "Of course, I have little access to any of the palaces."

"Neither do I," Jacob said. "Did you learn anything in Borsippa?"

"Not as much as I hoped," Ligish said. "Asher kept mostly to himself. He didn't have any close friends, and most of his acquaintances were other soldiers recruited from the Judean army."

"Asher was very careful about friendships," Jacob said. "Someone betrayed and hurt him in Jerusalem. It was before I met him. He never talked about it, but the scars were there, both on his body and in his head. Did you discover anything about Debra?"

Ligish shook his head, refilled Jacob's tankard, then his own. "Nothing specific. Like Gideon, some of those I spoke with sensed something was different with Asher after he came to help Arioch and me. They never said what was different, though."

Jacob thought about that for a while. "If those people are correct, my guess is that's about the time Asher met Debra. It could mean she's involved in this somehow."

"You didn't say it, but I sense you don't completely trust this woman, Debra. The one you're keeping safe."

Jacob sighed inside.

He knew Ligish was clever and picked up on words left unsaid. He had hoped the Babylonian wouldn't sense his uncertainty about Debra.

"There are enough inconsistencies in her story that I'm worried. It's likely she's still afraid and coming to terms with Asher's death. If she is involved, what does that tell you?" Jacob asked.

"Iddin," Ligish said without hesitation. "He's used your people before for his own ends. Nurval doesn't know enough about Babylon to involve anyone."

"Unless Debra came to Babylon with Nurval," Jacob said. "She's from the north, from what was the Northern Kingdom of Israel before the Assyrian invasion many years ago. I need to find out how and when she came to Babylon."

"You say she met Asher in Borsippa," Ligish said. "Do you want me to ask more questions there?"

Jacob thought for a moment, trying to decide if there was any benefit in sending Ligish back to Borsippa. Finally, he shook his head.

"I don't see we gain anything from it," he said. "We can't do anything about Nurval until Miriam returns from the Summer Palace, so Iddin is next. How do I approach him?"

"With me," Ligish said. "If you go alone, there's a strong possibility we'll be burying you beside Asher, and I don't want to answer to Miriam for that."

Jacob sat back on the bench, the tankard of beer cradled in his left hand, rested his head against the rough mud-brick wall.

Gideon had said much the same to him not three days ago.

Was he so consumed with finding Asher's killers that he was acting recklessly and without thought for his own safety? He didn't think so, but perhaps he needed time to think this through properly.

And with none of Gideon's beer in his stomach to cloud his mind.

It was too late to have those thoughts today. Jacob took a mouthful of the beer. There was another subject he could discuss with Ligish.

"Maybe we should leave Iddin for another day," he said. "Tell me more about Subisha. I'm hearing things about him that don't match with what you and Bel Ibni told me."

Ligish frowned, reached for the jug, and found it empty. He frowned again, said. "I'm not sure I understand."

Jacob took the empty jug from Ligish. He pulled the curtain to one side, saw the laborers were still at their table, and that more tables had people at them. He caught the attention of the serving girl, asked for the jug to be filled.

When the jug and their tankards were full again, Jacob said. "You tell me Subisha is ambitious, but our priest, Ezra, has met him. He tells me of a man dedicated to his gods."

"Why can't he be both?" Ligish asked.

"No reason," Jacob said. "Except Ezra compared Subisha to our prophet Jeremiah, and Jeremiah had no ambition for the high offices of the priesthood."

"Arioch knows and respects Ezra," Ligish said. "I also met him once. What does Ezra mean about your prophet Jeremiah?"

"Jeremiah sees the world differently than you and I do, and interprets it differently. He warned Judah what would happen if we continued ignoring Yahweh, and avoided several attempts at murder. It's like he has different priorities in his head."

Ligish was quiet for a long time. Long enough for Jacob to sip through half his tankard of beer.

"I think I know what you mean," Ligish said finally. "There are many occasions where Arioch has expressed frustration that Subisha does not understand the realities and constraints of his position. You recall I told you how Subisha helped save the temple herds during the drought?

"He did it with no consideration for how much gold and silver it took. It caused a lot of upsets in the temple, although the shepherds loved him for it. After that, the High Priest assigned Makru as his assistant," he smiled. "Probably to keep better track of the money."

"I don't expect you to agree, but hear me out first," Jacob said, pleased at the admission from Ligish.

"If Subisha truly is like Jeremiah, then his passion to be the high priest is false. That means someone wants everyone to believe Subisha seeks high office."

"Who?"

Jacob shook his head. "I don't know the workings of the Esagila well enough to make a guess. The other consideration is whoever this person is, what do they want, and why are they trying to destroy Arioch?"

"Power," Ligish said without hesitation. "If you manipulate Subisha, and replace Arioch with someone beholden to you, you can influence and control nearly every aspect of how the Esagila operates."

Ligish took a long swallow of his beer, shook his head. In the flickering light of the sesame oil lamp, his face looked haggard and drawn. "I can give you the names of three people who come to mind immediately. Probably three or four more with a little thought."

"Did you have this discussion with Asher?" Jacob asked, aware the list of people potentially involved with Asher's death had just two or three times.

Ligish shook his head again. "No. We talked mostly about Iddin, and some about Nurval."

"Either of them could own the person manipulating Subisha," Jacob said, then raised his hand to forestall Ligish. "If that's what is happening."

Ligish gave a harsh bark of a laugh. He reached for the jug, swore when he found it empty. He hefted the jug in his hand, made to pull the curtain aside, changed his mind, and set the jug back on the table with a thud.

"I am strongly tempted to indulge the desire to drink away my problems, even though I know it doesn't work," he said. "Do you have any suggestions, Jacob?"

"I've changed my mind," Jacob said. "Let me talk to Gideon and have him set someone to watch over Samuel and Rachel. Then, let's visit Iddin."

CHAPTER FOURTEEN

The seventh day of Abu - Afternoon

The floors in the hallways of the Summer Palace were paved with enormous blocks of white stone that echoed the noise of Miriam's sandals as she made her way up three long flights of steps toward the rooms occupied by the Judean nobles.

The walls on the stairways and along the hallways were covered with elaborate and expensive tapestries. Miriam guessed each tapestry celebrated an event during Nebuchadnezzar's reign. She was grateful she saw nothing that looked like the siege and sack of Jerusalem.

Around her, the gentle movement of cooler air kept the heat at a pleasant and bearable level, and she caught the faint scent of flowers in the moving air. Miriam remembered Jacob telling her Nebuchadnezzar had constructed special shafts that cooled the air in the palace. This walk must be a blessing for Esther, she thought, as her cousin didn't do well in the baking heat of Babylonian summers.

Esther walked on Miriam's right-hand side. Miriam glanced at her cousin, relieved to see Esther looked flushed, but not uncomfortable. The two priests assigned by Ezra walked three or four paces ahead, although the hallway was wide enough they could all walk side-by-side if they wished.

"Why am I here with you, Miriam?" Esther asked as they passed the gleaming bronze statues of a pair of lions, and two servants hurrying in the opposite direction.

"The servants are better dressed than we are."

Miriam plucked at the sleeve of her emerald green robe. Her best robe.

"Which is why I wanted your support," she said. "It's possible some women we meet will recognize me as Nahum's wife. If you are with me, I hope there is less chance of questions."

"I hope so too," Esther said. She waved her arm in a sweeping gesture that took in the hallway's length with all the ornaments and decorations.

"Does this remind you of the Temple in Jerusalem?"

Miriam glanced around, considered Esther's words. "If you mean the extravagance, and the amount of silver and gold needed for the tapestries, and statues, and everything else, then yes, it does. Too much so. It's not a comparison I enjoy," she said, keeping her voice low so the priests ahead wouldn't hear her words.

They turned a corner, and before Esther could reply, Miriam saw Ezra standing by a doorway waiting for them.

Ezra spoke to the shorter of the two priests in a low voice Miriam couldn't hear. The man nodded, turned and hurried past Miriam and Esther. Miriam tried not to shake her head. He looked barely more than a boy, his chin smooth with no signs of beard growth.

She looked at Ezra, who smiled, shrugged his shoulders.

"He will watch for Nurval, and I know. They get younger and younger. In a few years, we will have priests who never knew the Temple, and we will lose another piece of our heritage."

"We had faith before King Solomon built the Temple," Miriam said. "Perhaps those pieces of heritage we lose are pieces we should have lost many years ago."

His dark eyes went wide.

For a moment, Miriam feared she had offended Ezra. Then his face lit up. He smiled, nearly laughed, took her hands in his.

"I almost feel sorry for Jacob if he ever tries arguing with you," then his face lost its humor. "Suri is not doing well with the heat. I am told she has another two moons before the child arrives, but I believe you may think differently."

Miriam felt her heart beat a little faster. She looked over to Esther, and for once there was no readable expression on her cousin's face.

"I've helped deliver babies, Ezra, but I never trained as a midwife. I don't know I can, or should, go against their advice."

"Then just talk to Suri," Ezra said. "She's tired of being poked and pulled and not being told what the answers are. Or even if there are any."

"That I understand," Miriam said. She took Esther's arm, stepped round Ezra, and entered the room.

The cooling air that flowed through the hallways didn't follow them into the room. Miriam felt the heat immediately, felt the perspiration bead on her face, heard the sharp intake of breath that signaled the first sign of Esther's discomfort.

Suri, the pregnant woman, girl really, Miriam thought. She doubted Suri was older than sixteen years. Maybe not even that.

The girl lay on a divan on the far side of the room. Her face was flushed scarlet, her breath coming in quick gasps as she wiped a damp cloth over her face.

She wore an off-white under a dress that rippled and shifted as the baby moved inside her.

Two moons until the birth, Ezra had said.

As Miriam crossed the room, she studied the size and shape of Suri's distended belly, saw how low the baby was positioned.

Small wonder Suri was uncomfortable.

Miriam guessed Suri had only a moon before the birth, if that long.

Suri took a long shallow breath, opened her eyes, turned her head, and looked at Miriam

"You're the herbalist, aren't you?" Suri said in a soft, breathy voice. "The one who was married to a priest."

So much for avoiding questions, Miriam thought and braced herself for the many questions she expected to follow."

She started in surprise when she recognized the next voice.

"Yes, Miriam was married to a priest," Esther said. "He died on the trek into Exile, and in my opinion, no loss. It was hard on my cousin, but she's come through it all the stronger."

There was an awkward silence as everyone looked at her. Looks that made Miriam wish the floor could open and swallow her up.

Instead, Suri let out a breathy laugh. "I wish I had family that loyal?"

She waved her arm, beckoned Miriam to come closer.

"What do you think, Miriam? Do I have to bear this for another two moons?"

"One at the outside," Miriam said. "Possibly much sooner."

Suri laughed again, although it was breathless and seemed to drain away more of her energy. She ignored the surprised looks on the faces of the women around her, and pointed at one of them; a slender woman with shoulder length hair the color of ripe chestnuts.

"Someone who agrees with you, Leah. The two of you should talk," Suri said, then let herself slide back on the couch like the effort had been too much for her.

Leah crossed the room as the other women clustered once more around Suri or returned to their needlework. She didn't speak until she was close beside Miriam.

"I knew of your husband," Leah said in a low voice that was deeper and richer than Miriam expected.

"His death was no loss to the Temple, and I suspect a release and relief for you."

Miriam chose her words carefully. She didn't know these women, had no insight into their thoughts and connections with the other Exiles.

"It took me a long time to come to terms with it," Miriam said.

"A careful answer," Leah said with a smile that reached her hazel eyes and revealed a small dimple on her chin. "Do you really believe it will be as long as a month before Suri gives birth?"

Miriam shook her head. "Look how low the baby has settled. If Suri began her labor tonight, it would not surprise me."

"It would not surprise me either and I'm not popular for saying it,"

Leah said. She gestured toward Miriam's bag. "Are you going to give her anything?"

"Something mild to help her relax, and maybe to sleep," Miriam said. "I don't want to risk the child at this stage."

"Have either of you delivered a baby?"

"Only my two boys," Esther said.

"None of my own, but I've helped," Miriam said.

Leah nodded. Miriam wasn't sure if it meant approval or acceptance. Leah inclined her head to indicate the other women.

"They're good souls, but none of them have any idea about birthing a child. Or what to do when one arrives. I'd feel much more comfortable if another of our people were with me. Miriam, would you consider staying here to help?"

"At another time, I would say yes without reservation," Miriam said. "For now, I must say no, for reasons I cannot speak of. I understand this is Suri's first child. In my experience, it's unlikely her labor will be fast."

Leah started to respond as Ezra came into the room. His dark brown eyes tracked across the space, skipped Suri and her attendants. He focused on Miriam and gave her a nod.

"I see you have other reasons for being in the Summer Palace," Leah said. "Leave me the soothing herbs you mentioned and I'll make sure Suri gets them."

Miriam opened the bag on her shoulder, fingered through the contents, and picked out two packages. One of rosemary, the other chamomile. She handed the packages to Leah.

"Let these steep in separate mugs of hot water for a long count of three hundred, then make sure Suri drinks everything. When she begins her labor, send for me at the house of Isaac and Esther. I will come as quickly as I can."

Leah folded her fingers round Miriam's hand, glanced at Ezra, then looked back to Miriam. "Do what you have to do, and know that you can trust me. I will send for you when it is Suri's time. Perhaps after the child is born, we can talk openly, and you will understand why you can trust me."

"I'd like that," Miriam said, surprised at how much she meant it.

Miriam turned away, saw Esther was already beside Ezra, that both of them had impatient looks on their faces.

"Quickly, or you will miss the chance," Ezra said, almost pushing them out of the room and along the hallway, back the way they had come earlier in the day.

Ezra continued straight on past hallways on the left and right. His robe billowed, his graying hair spiked and unruly.

Eventually, they came out onto a covered walkway with a waist-high wall. Three stories below them, Miriam saw gardens richer and lusher than anything she had seen since leaving Jerusalem. The musical tinkle of water in fountains came to her, along with the delicate fragrance of lime trees, lemon trees, jasmine blossom.

And roses.

Miriam wondered how easy it would be to grow roses at the house Jacob was building. With roses, she could make rose oil for skin care and the relief of tension. And she could try mixing the roses with lavender and other herbs.

Miriam wished she had time to sit and enjoy the assault on her senses, but Ezra had increased his pace. Already Esther was almost running, trying to keep up. Miriam lengthened her stride to catch them.

Ahead, and coming toward them, was a group of five people, and behind them a clerk, moving quickly, head down so Miriam could only see his dark, almost black hair. His arms were full of a stack of papyrus scrolls he struggled to keep balanced.

One figure stood out in the main group. A man, a head or two taller than everyone else.

Miriam knew he must be Nurval. Beside Nurval was a woman in a flowing blue robe with chestnut hair flowing down nearly to her waist. Around them, three servants carried packages.

Nurval and the woman, Miriam assumed she was his wife, were engaged in an animated conversation. It wasn't an argument yet, but the tone of their voices reached her, and she knew it could be soon.

They were less than twenty paces from Nurval. Ezra stepped forward when Nurval's raised voice came to them. Raised in anger, or at least frustration, Miriam thought.

"Absolutely not!" Nurval said, loud, but not quite loud enough to echo along the hallway. "We all know Iddin is a thug. It's how he grew up."

Ezra paused in mid-stride.

Two paces ahead of Miriam, Esther let out a gasp of horror.

Miriam followed Esther's gaze.

The clerk had shifted from a fast walk to a run. The scrolls were discarded, tumbling to the surrounding tiles. His body was squat and muscular, pushing him forward. The long dagger that had appeared in his right hand glinted and flashed in the light. He shoved past the servants, elbowed Nurval's wife in the abdomen. She stumbled to the side, screamed as the knife stabbed and slashed into Nurval's body.

As Nurval fell, his wife screamed again, covered her mouth with her hands, her eyes wide.

Miriam saw the look in the wife's brown eyes. Recognized it now as the same look she had seen in Ruth's eyes the previous day.

Fear.

Why was Ruth afraid?

Miriam had no time to think about Ruth.

The attacker pushed away from Nurval, ducked his head to avoid the wife's grab, slipped on a puddle of spilled blood.

Miriam ran forward, reached the killer as he put a bloodied hand on the wall to pull himself up. She kicked his hand off the wall, wincing at the sharp pain in the unprotected upper part of her foot. He slipped to the floor again. Miriam dropped onto his back. She slammed his head onto the tile floor. The knife clattered away. His body went limp.

The wife continued her screams until Esther stepped over Nurval's body and gave her a firm slap on the cheek.

The noise stopped. The servants stood in stunned silence, their faces pale with shock.

And then the noise began again.

The crash of booted feet on the tiled floor. Shouts and bellowed orders.

The palace guards had arrived. Miriam barely had time to register it all before hands grabbed her arms, dragged her roughly to her feet. Blood smeared across her robe, and she felt a surge of anger.

Why was it every piece of good clothing she owned became ripped, torn, or stained?

Miriam tried to struggle. The hands holding her gripped tighter. She knew she'd have marks on her arms after this.

One of the guard officers came toward her. She saw his mouth move, but with all the surrounding noise, his Akkadian came across garbled and impossible to understand.

When she didn't answer, he scowled, lifted his arm to strike her.

"No!" Nurval's wife said, her shrill voice cutting through the noise. "She helped. That's why the man who murdered my husband is laying there before you."

The guard officer lowered his arm, barked an order, and Miriam felt the pressure on her arms go away. She stepped to the side, used her hands to massage her upper arms, could feel the indentations where the soldier's fingers had dug into her skin. Miriam hoped there was still some of the yarrow salve she had made to ease the bruises Esther's boys seemed to gain every day.

A scuffle of movement and Esther's squeak of horror pulled Miriam out of her thoughts.

The nearest guard rolled the killer over onto his back. As the man rolled, he dragged a short knife from inside his boot and drove it into the guard's calf.

The guard collapsed with a whimper.

The killer lurched to his feet. There was blood on his temple from where Miriam had driven his head onto the tile. He wiped the blood away. His dark eyes flickered as he took in the hallway, took in everyone surrounding him, focused on Miriam.

He closed his eyes for a moment, took a long breath.

The murderer lifted his hand in salute to Miriam, took two steps, and a long dive over the railing into the gardens three stories below.

____

CHAPTER FIFTEEN

____

The seventh day of Abu - Afternoon

Jacob gasped as he followed Ligish out of the tavern into the brutal afternoon heat on the side street. He kept his breathing shallow so he couldn't taste the smell of rotting refuse and followed Ligish onto Sin Street.

Normally, Jacob preferred the secondary streets of the city, and avoided Babylon's major thoroughfares as much as he could. Ligish, possibly because of his rank, and the imposing sight of his ornate temple guard uniform, seemed to prefer those major thoroughfares.

Ligish led the way along Sin Street to the end, then right along Marduk Street toward the Esagila.

There were slow-moving crowds at the end of Marduk Street where it joined the Processional Way, right in front of the Esagila. It was the usual assortment of merchants and pilgrims pushing, shoving and jostling each other. Jacob was content to follow as Ligish pushed a path through the crowds.

Crowds like this are why I use the smaller streets, Jacob thought as an elbow caught him in the ribs, and he narrowly avoided the snapping jaws of a female goat, who decided he was too close or too tasty to miss. He tapped the doe on her nose with the flat of his hand. She shied away, bleating in protest as Jacob continued past. Then he realized Ligish had stopped by the side of the street, and was talking to a member of the temple guard.

The noise of the people and animals around him prevented Jacob from hearing the conversation. He saw the blue sash over the man's uniform tunic. His stomach did a nervous flip.

The soldier was a member of the temple guard stationed at the Summer Palace to carry messages between the palace and the Esagila.

When the conversation was over, Ligish placed his hand on the man's shoulder, said something in a low tone, which again Jacob couldn't hear.

The messenger gave a quick salute, and moved away, back north along the Processional Way toward the Ishtar Gate.

Ligish turned to Jacob, his face grim. Jacob felt his stomach flip again. The aftertaste of the beer in his mouth was sour and bitter.

"What happened?" he asked, afraid of the answer.

Ligish moved them both closer to the side of the street, away from the heavy press of people.

"Someone attacked and killed Nurval," Ligish said, then shook his head and allowed a wide grin to split his face.

"It happened in front of Miriam, and she prevented the murderer from escaping. That was until the palace guard stopped paying attention and he jumped from a balcony three stories high rather than remain a captive."

"Miriam?"

"Is fine. And no, we are not going to the palace," Ligish said, his hand on Jacob's shoulder to restrain him.

Jacob considered breaking free. It was a simple move and wouldn't hurt Ligish.

Ligish must have sensed Jacob's mood. His grip tightened. His voice became low and insistent.

"I have trouble getting into any of the palaces at the best of times. After this event, I have no chance, and if you try, you'll end up in one of their cells. You don't want that experience."

Jacob took a long breath, knowing in his head Ligish was right, still not liking it though. The thought took him back to his days as a soldier. He had said something very similar to Gideon on the walls of Jerusalem during the last days of the siege.

Jacob nodded, felt the grip on his shoulder ease, then disappear.

"I need to talk with Arioch," Ligish said. "You'd best come with me. I'm sure Miriam will be at Isaac's home when we are done."

"You should be with me at Isaac's," Jacob said, forcing his voice to sound normal, and his mind to focus on something other than his fear for Miriam. "We might both learn something from her story."

"A good idea," Ligish said, and led the way across the Processional Way into the Esagila.

The rows of clerks and scribes working outside Arioch's office barely lifted their heads, or acknowledged their presence, as Jacob and Ligish walked between the rows of desks.

If news of Nurval's murder had reached them, they appeared unaffected.

Ligish reached the doors to Arioch's office, rapped his knuckles on the polished cedar, and pushed through without waiting for a response.

The office looked to Jacob much as it had when he was there four days ago. The details on the waxed covered boards had changed, but the boards remained on the wall facing the windows overlooking the Esagila courtyard.

There was no sign of the cat.

Arioch sat in a chair at the low table in the middle of the room. Beside Arioch, Jacob recognized the priest who officiated at the wedding of Horam and Damkina. A priest with a future, Arioch had told Jacob. A man to watch.

Opposite Arioch was another priest with an assistant sat beside him. The priest was a squat portly man, and even sitting, Jacob could see he was a good head shorter than Arioch. His hair was a ring of thin brown wisps that looked like an insecure crown. The assistant was leaner, taller, with a feral look in his dark brown eyes.

All four looked toward the door as Jacob, and Ligish entered. The scowl on Arioch's face revealed his displeasure.

"Please forgive the intrusion," Ligish said. "I have just received information from the Summer Palace for excellency, Arioch."

"This information cannot wait, Ligish?"

Ligish shook his head. "Unfortunately, no, or I would not have interrupted your meeting."

Arioch sighed, pushed to his feet, spoke to the other priest. "Think about what I've proposed, Subisha. We can discuss it further this evening."

"Priest Subisha has his meditation this evening," the assistant said, his voice rough like his throat had been damaged at some time in the past.

"Yes. That's right, I do. Thank you, Makru," Subisha said, sounding like he had just woken from a deep sleep. "Can we discuss this again tomorrow, Arioch? After Makru and I have time to fully review the proposal."

"That will be acceptable," Arioch said.

Jacob knew from Arioch's tone, the priest considered it anything but acceptable. He stood to one side, near the window where soft wind stirred the air, making it feel cooler but not really providing relief from the heat. As the others gathered scrolls and tablets and filed from the room, Makru looked over at Jacob.

There was contempt in the man's eyes.

Makru looked about to say something, then seemed to think better of it.

"What is it that's so important it cannot wait?" Arioch asked when the doors were closed and it was just the three of them in the room.

"It has taken me weeks to get Subisha to discuss a better way to feed the herds during the winter. It will take more weeks to get him to sit down again. By then, autumn will be on us and we risk the herds."

"You need to be aware of this news," Ligish said. "Jacob and I met a messenger on our way here. An assassin killed Nurval in the Summer Palace earlier this afternoon. The knife he carried has the markings of the Esagila."

Arioch dropped back into his chair, ran a hand over the sharp angles of his face. "There are many knives with Esagila markings," he said. "As many outside the temple as inside. It doesn't mean the assassin came from here."

He looked to have aged ten years since Jacob entered the room.

Arioch closed his eyes, tilted his head back, and said. "Do you think this is related to Asher and our other problems, Jacob?"

Jacob stepped away from the window. "It's a convenient coincidence," he said. "And I don't think you should ignore the knife. If it were me, I'd spread a story of disagreement and arguments between Nurval and the temple of Marduk, and how the temple found him difficult to deal with."

"We barely talk with him," Ligish said. "He sends his assistants to negotiate with us."

"You're both right," Arioch said, sitting forward. "Nurval has always dealt with us at one remove. It's just the way he is. Was. Unfortunately, that helps the story Jacob would spread."

Arioch came to his feet, paced the length of the room twice, then a third time. He paused in front of the waxed boards, but Jacob doubted Arioch was seeing any of the information before him. Finally, he turned back to face Jacob and Ligish.

"I will go to the Summer Palace and represent the Esagila. It may not prevent the rumors, but is not unexpected given our trade with Nurval and his partners. We'll also send an envoy to Haran."

Arioch looked at Jacob. There was a thin smile on his face, although no humor. "I may be able to help if the palace guard are being difficult about Miriam."

Ligish looked conflicted, and Jacob knew why. "Your place is with Arioch," he said. "Let's meet here tomorrow morning, and I can tell you everything I learned from Miriam before we visit Iddin."

Ligish looked about to protest, then his body relaxed. "We can compare what we learned. I may learn something more by being with Arioch."

Jacob saw the shift in Ligish then, from concerned friend to head of the temple guard.

As Jacob let himself out of the room, he heard the two Babylonians discuss who to send to Haran.

CHAPTER SIXTEEN

The seventh day of Abu - Evening

The sun was low in the western sky when Miriam and Esther came through the crowds at the Ishtar Gate and onto the stone slabs that paved the Processional Way.

Esther looked flushed and flustered as Miriam pushed through the mules, carts, and press of people into one of the side streets.

Miriam was ready to lengthen her stride, walk faster along the less-traveled side streets when Esther called out, her voice breathless.

"Miriam, why are you in such a hurry?"

She paused at Esther's question, stepped to the side of the street, turned, and waited for her cousin to catch up.

She offered a prayer of thanks that no-one seemed to pay them any attention. When Esther reached her, Miriam said.

"We saw something terrible today. I will never forget the look on his wife's face. I don't want to miss Shema. Not tonight."

Esther sucked in a trio of ragged breaths, then tipped her head.

"You're more like your father than you care to admit," Esther said

She put her hand on Miriam's arm. "I mean that in a good way,

Miriam, and after this afternoon, I think I understand. Evening prayer will calm us both, maybe even help us sleep."

Esther looked up at the sky, the fading light now. The sun was lower than the city walls.

"We'll be there in time," she said, and set off without waiting.

Miriam smiled, and followed, grateful her cousin understood without expecting any more explanation.

Oil lamps flickered in the courtyard of Isaac's home, adding pools of bright light and the nutty scent of sesame as the last light of the day faded.

Isaac, a prayer shawl over his shoulders, looked about to say something, then changed his mind. He waited while Miriam and Esther regained their breath. When they showed they were ready, he began.

Miriam felt the cadence of Isaac's voice, the rhythm of the words wash over her. She took a long breath before speaking the responses, and praise be, her voice was stronger than she expected.

When the prayers were finished, and Esther's sons had greeted their mother properly, Miriam said to Esther. "I need to change this robe."

Esther gave her a sympathetic smile. "I know, and don't worry, we'll get it clean. I'll make sure there's wine ready when you come back down."

Miriam smiled, couldn't help herself.

"That would be most welcome," she said.

She was barely halfway across the courtyard, to the outside stairs that led to the upper balcony, and her room, when there was a commotion at the door.

Miriam turned, saw Jacob push past Solly. He came at her in a wild rush. She barely had time to brace herself before his arms were round her and she was crushed against his chest.

His words when he spoke were breathless, and he couldn't keep the emotion from them. "I was with Ligish when a messenger arrived. I've been afraid for you."

What a welcome, Miriam thought.

It was as well Esther and Isaac no longer expected anyone to chaperone them, or his actions would have been unacceptable.

"I am well enough," Miriam said, lifting her head off his chest, seeing the concern and worry in his brown eyes.

"A bruised foot, and another robe ruined," she said. "Give me some time to find a clean robe, and while I do that, please make sure Esther makes good on her promise of wine."

She felt the rumble of the laughter in his chest, which choked off when she heard Esther's voice.

"Why do you never greet me like that, Isaac?"

Miriam laughed herself, and again as Isaac, surprised, stuttered and stammered an attempted reply.

She felt Jacob's arms release her. He stepped back, and immediately Miriam missed the contact, wanting to step back and nestle against his body for the rest of the evening.

She took a quick breath, firmed her resolve, reached up and touched his cheek.

"I won't be long," she said, lifted the hem of her robe, and almost ran up the steps.

The robe Miriam chose was the first she found: an older one used for helping Esther with cleaning. It was patched and repaired in several places; the hem frayed with loose threads dangling. For a moment, Miriam considered something else, then realized Jacob would see this robe, and others like it, after they were married. It wouldn't all be fine dressing.

If she was honest with herself, she hoped the times for fine dressing would be few.

The look Jacob sent her when she reached the table told Miriam she had made the right choice. His eyes were for her, not what she wore.

And, praise be, he had a goblet of wine that she accepted gratefully, and took a long swallow.

Miriam sat on the couch beside Jacob, the boys opposite, Isaac and Esther at each end of the table. The food steamed on the table before them. A stew, barley bread, and surprisingly a platter with what smelled like chicken.

She looked a question at Esther. Sitting on her left.

"After the day we've had, I thought some meat was deserved,"

Esther said. "Mind you, it may taste like the sole of your sandal. It wasn't a young chicken."

"Right now, the sole of my sandal is looking like a good meal," Miriam said, and lifted her goblet to thank Esther.

Isaac and Jacob kept the conversation light during the meal. Miriam could feel the nervous tension in Jacob, and the many questions Isaac almost asked, then glanced at his sons and changed his mind.

These were not questions for young ears.

When the meal was finished, Esther instructed the boys to follow the servants who would see them to bed. Then she stood and poured more wine, even though her cheeks were already flushed.

"If we keep having days like this, the boys will have to eat in the kitchen," Isaac said as Esther returned to her seat.

"Absolutely not. The boys eat with us," Esther said.

Miriam caught the sharp edge in Esther's voice, sensed the quirk of a smile on Jacob's face, that he hid by turning away.

Her cousin had mellowed over the past months, and Miriam liked Esther all the more for that mellowing. Still, she was pleased Esther's tongue kept its sharp edge.

"As you wish," Isaac said. "Now, please tell us what happened at the Summer Palace this afternoon."

"I'll let Esther correct me if I tell anything wrong," Miriam said. She took a sip of wine and related the events of Nurval's murder.

When she finished, Esther shook her head, said. "I'm still not sure I believe I saw the man jump to his death. What would make someone do that?"

Miriam looked at Jacob, who shrugged. "Belief in a cause. Or the knowledge that failure would mean a painful death, perhaps for his family as well. The Assyrian king Tiglath-Peleser bound his bodyguards in that way. Any betrayal or failure meant execution for the guard and his family."

"Did the man who killed Nurval look like a soldier?" Miriam asked Esther.

Esther thought for a moment, then shook her head. "More like a ruffian."

"The people who lead or control ruffians work similarly," Jacob said. "They demand complete loyalty and are ruthless and brutal with failure or betrayal."

"Which brings you no closer to learning who killed Asher, or who wants to remove Arioch," Isaac said. He reached for the wine jug and refilled all the goblets.

Miriam saw the grimace on Jacob's face at Isaac's words. They both knew Isaac was correct with his observation, but she would prefer a more positive comment.

"What are your plans?" Miriam asked Jacob.

"This talk of ruffians is appropriate," he said. "Ligish and I are going to visit Iddin tomorrow. He is trying hard to become an honest merchant and trader, but I wonder if control of the business in the Esagila isn't more to his liking. How was the mother-to-be? Suri wasn't it?"

"Closer to being a mother than most people are expecting," Miriam said, and with Esther's contributions, told about the earlier, happier part of their visit to the Summer Palace.

Later, after Jacob had left, and Miriam lay on her bed, trying to calm her mind again so she could sleep, she remembered she hadn't told Jacob about Ruth.

CHAPTER SEVENTEEN

The eighth day of Abu - Morning

The following morning, after a solitary Shema, Jacob made his way to the Esagila to meet Ligish. Clouds had come in from the east overnight, leaving the morning light dull, the sky gray and overcast. The clouds brought an oppressive, humid feel to the air that made even the lightest clothes feel heavy and uncomfortable.

There was a storm coming, and Jacob wished it would hurry. The storm would clear the air, even if there was no rain with it. He welcomed the prospect of rain, no matter how little fell. It would be warm and soaking, but at least it would remove the dry, oppressive heat for a few days, maybe long enough for an early start to the cooler fall weather.

The unpleasant weather had thinned the crowds of merchants, traders, and pilgrims around the Esagila, and Jacob had no trouble crossing the Processional Way to the main gate of the temple complex where he saw Ligish waiting.

Ligish wore his full temple guard uniform without the helmet or cloak. He looked miserable in the heavy cloth tunic and leather breastplate. There was a grim look on his face, and on the faces of the two guardsmen standing beside him.

Jacob gestured at the guardsmen. "I know you said visiting Iddin on my own was a bad idea, but do we need the formal dress and escort?"

"This may be more than a visit," Ligish said.

Close to, Jacob could see the dark lines etched under Ligish's sunken and hollowed eyes, and the way he held himself like every muscle ached. Jacob suspected the Babylonian had slept little last night.

"Arioch and I recognized the man who murdered Nurval," Ligish continued. "His name was Sadudu, one of Iddin's men. Well respected by Iddin if my sources are correct, and a man who spent a lot of time in the Esagila. Are you ready?"

Jacob wished he had another hour or two. The extra time would let him talk with Gideon and confirm what Ligish said about Sadudu.

He saw the way the guards shifted their feet, fidgeted with their belts and equipment. Saw the impatience on Ligish's face.

There was no extra time if he wanted to visit Iddin with Ligish.

"I'm ready," Jacob said. "While we walk, I'll tell you what I learned from Miriam, although I think it may be less than you already know or suspect."

Jacob had visited the west side of Babylon on many occasions. The area had been built after the main city on the east bank and was referred to as the New Town.

The houses, taverns, and temples felt crowded to Jacob. They were too close together. The two and three-story buildings loomed over the streets, dulling the light even further, and trapping the heat. Everything about the area made Jacob feel uncomfortable.

The attention they attracted in the narrow streets did not help his mood. Onlookers and passersby watched them with a mix of emotions. Some frightened, some hostile, and occasionally a glance of sympathy toward Jacob like he was caught up in something beyond his control, and against his will.

Iddin's home was on the edge of the Tuba ward near the Shamash gate on the southwestern side of the city. The house was a three story building at the end of a short street. Jacob estimated the rear of the house merged into the city walls. The arrangement gave Iddin a route out of the city, should he ever need to escape from Babylon.

Ligish announced their business to the two guards outside a main door that looked to be made of solid cedar. The guards made them wait outside, then insisted only Jacob and Ligish could enter.

Inside the door was a poorly lit, hot and airless storage floor. The guard led them up two flights of stairs to a more open area with light coming in from tall windows on the wall opposite the stairs.

A long couch was on the left-hand side, with Iddin sat on it, looking relaxed. Two more guards stood behind the couch, obscuring a brightly colored tapestry that hung along the full length of the wall. There was a low table in front of the couch with clay tablets and papyrus scrolls strewn across it in a haphazard pattern. Beside the table was a trio of small stools built for children rather than adults.

Another staircase led to the next level. Jacob heard the shrill chatter and laughter of young girls from the upper rooms, caught the tang of wood smoke, and the smell of meat roasting. Goat, he guessed.

There were cabinets against the wall behind him, and more of the brightly colored tapestries. The furniture made the room seem smaller than it really was.

If the situation became violent, there was barely room to wield a sword. The weapon Ligish had strapped to his waist would be useless. Not for the first time, Jacob wished he'd had the foresight to strap a weapon to his right forearm, the way Miriam did with a bone needle.

Iddin watched them enter the room. His dark eyes showed no emotion, his thin, almost skeletal features impassive.

He made no attempt at hospitality. Jacob recognized the behavior as the insult Iddin intended it to be.

"I suppose you're here to talk about Sadudu." Iddin said, his voice a low growl.

"We are." Ligish barely kept the surprise from his voice.

The statement made sense to Jacob. Iddin had a reputation for keeping close control of the people who worked for him.

"I would be a liar if I said I'm disappointed not to give you what you want. Sadudu is no longer in my employ. I dismissed him three or four moons ago for stealing."

Jacob worked hard to keep the laughter from his voice. "Stealing?"
He wasn't sure he succeeded

Iddin scowled, gave a long sigh. "I'm sure it amuses you no end, Jacob. Let me explain. There are many people who don't have the safety of the temple stipend, or the benefit of some noble patron. Many of them struggle to find food, especially the children. I know this because it's how I grew up, and it helped make me who I am."

Iddin raised his hand about waist high, palm down. "I was this high when I vowed I would do something for the people in my village. I send grain, beans, and vegetables every week. It's not much, but it stops them from starving.

"Sadudu decided he would take a seventh for himself. A few years ago, I would have dropped him into the Euphrates. He's fortunate all he received was a beating, and my foot when I kicked him out."

"Who was Sadudu working for when he went to the palace?" Ligish asked.

Iddin shook his head. "I don't know. In a way, I was hoping you might give me some information about him. I like to keep track of my former employees so I have warning if they develop some misguided ideas about revenge. Sadudu just disappeared."

"Do you have any thoughts on how Sadudu got into the Summer Palace?" Ligish asked.

Iddin laughed, a harsh, high-pitched bark. "Ligish, what makes you think I have any way to get into the Summer Palace? And before you ask, yes, I met with Nurval frequently, but never at the Palace. There was no chance of getting approval for me to be there, so we met here or at the caravan grounds. Mostly the caravan grounds, because Nurval doesn't like enclosed spaces."

"Why were you meeting?" Jacob asked.

Iddin's face went still, like he didn't want to answer the question. After a long pause, Iddin gestured toward the clay tablets on the table in front of him.

"Nurval and I were negotiating a business agreement. I have a tablet, signed and sealed with witnesses. It appoints me as Nurval's agent in Babylon to buy and sell on his behalf. What will come of the agreement now? I don't know."

Iddin sighed, ran a hand through hair as dark as his eyes. "Where is the benefit to me of having Nurval murdered?"

He fixed Ligish with a hard stare, and his black eyes glittered. "Perhaps you would be better served looking inside the temple rather than make accusations with nothing to support them."

Jacob thought Ligish looked embarrassed. Jacob knew he would have felt that way if it were him, and he felt sympathy for Ligish. If the agreement with Nurval survived, Iddin could become a regular visitor to the Esagila. It would not serve Ligish well to have Iddin as an adversary.

"My apologies," Ligish said. "My sources of information appear to be lacking. I take your point about the temple. On a related subject, there are many temple rules, some of which I suspect date back to the first Nebuchadnezzar. Some rules disagree with each other, and can make it very difficult to achieve your goals. If you wish, I can help you work round some of the less sensible rules."

Iddin sat back in his chair, stroked at his beard. As the moment stretched, Jacob felt a twist in his stomach, becoming more certain Iddin would refuse the offer.

Jacob hoped Iddin refused the offer with tact.

And then Iddin smiled and sat forward, gave a curt nod. "That is a kind offer."

Iddin turned to the nearest guard. "Have wine brought in. And proper chairs for my guests."

After the chairs arrived, and the wine poured, Iddin said to Jacob. "I understand your woman, Miriam had a part in capturing Sadudu."

"She stopped him from escaping," Jacob said. "After that, he broke free from the palace guards and jumped from a high walkway."

Iddin shook his head. "You Judeans allow your women a freedom I'm not sure is wise. Perhaps that's why you are exiled to Babylon rather than hosting us as exiles in Jerusalem."

"It's possible," Jacob said. He sipped at his wine, which was surprisingly good, and ignored the twinkle of amusement in Ligish's eyes.

"Do you have any idea why Sadudu would kill himself?" Ligish asked.

"Obviously, he wasn't supposed to be caught," Iddin said, then barked out another laugh. "Whoever Sadudu worked for had a powerful hold over him. I've never seen that level of loyalty or commitment."

He shrugged. "I don't ask for it either."

The tension in the room had eased, and the conversation turned to other subjects, the barley crops, those items selling well for traders, and the hope of rain with the storm.

After the wine was finished, Ligish pushed to his feet. Jacob joined him. It was best to offer thanks and leave while Iddin remained in good spirits.

As they reached the stairs leading to the lower level, Jacob turned back, said to Iddin. "Is there someone we can talk to who might know where Sadudu went after you dismissed him?"

Iddin paused in the act of refreshing his wine, favored Jacob with an ironic smile. "None of my people. Even if they knew, they won't admit it anywhere near me, and I won't allow you to talk to them alone. Sadudu came from the Te-Eki ward. Be careful if you go looking for information there. There are no temples in that part of the city. It's a rough area once you leave the safety of Enlil or Zababa Streets. After dark, I wouldn't call those streets safe. The people there care little for Marduk," he looked at Jacob. "Or Judeans."

"Thank you. I'll keep it in mind if I go there," Jacob said.

He knew he would make that journey. It might be the only chance he had left to learn who killed Asher. He had his foot on the first step when Iddin called out.

"Sadudu frequented a tavern at the corner of Enlil and Zababa Streets, close to the Enlil Gate. With the right incentives, they might be persuaded to tell you who he worked for."

<hr>

CHAPTER EIGHTEEN

<hr>

The eighth day of Abu - Afternoon

The messenger from the Summer Palace reached Miriam just after the midday meal. She was working on the prayer shawl for Jacob, and had two sets of knots left to complete the shawl when she was interrupted.

She had folded the shawl away carefully, packed her bag with herbs, salves, and pain remedies, and warned Esther not to expect her before the morning. Maybe even the day after that.

The guards at the Summer Palace were expecting her, and escorted her along the wide cool hallways to the same room she had been in the day before.

The couches and chairs Miriam had seen on her first visit were piled against the walls to one side of the room. In their place was the bed where Suri lay.

Miriam looked past Leah, seeing who else, apart from Suri, was in the room. She was surprised to see an older woman sitting by Suri's head on a stool. The profile looked familiar, and Miriam wasn't sure how she knew, but she was certain the woman wasn't a Judean.

"Where are Suri's family?" Miriam asked.

"Suri has no family of her own." Leah said. "Her parents and sisters died on the journey into Exile. What remains of her family is in Jerusalem. They weren't considered important enough to be taken into Exile. Her husband's family is more interested in attending a meal with King Zedekiah than helping bring their next generation into the world. I sent the other women away."

"I see why you wanted help," Miriam said. She gestured toward the woman sat by Suri's head.

"Who is that?"

The woman left off, wiping a damp cloth across Suri's forehead, and looked over at Miriam. The woman's long chestnut hair was pulled back into a tight ponytail. Her face looked tired and wan, and there were gray shadows under her eyes like she hadn't slept in a long time.

Probably not for nearly two days, Miriam thought. She gave Nurval's widow a nod of recognition. The woman inclined her head in return.

"I am Mylitta," she said. "The Summer Palace is a small world, and very little remains private for long. When I heard Suri had gone into labor, I came to help. It's better than sitting in my rooms alone, looking at the walls and thinking of my husband."

"I'm sorry I couldn't do more for him," Miriam said as Suri let out a cry of agony, her back arching off the bed, her eyes wide with pain.

Mylitta wiped a cloth over Suri's face again, held the girl's hand, and looked back to Miriam.

"You did more than anyone else. I am glad you're here. I wanted to find you and thank you for what you tried to do."

"Leave that conversation for later, when we're celebrating the birth of Suri's child," Leah said, waving Miriam to the opposite end of the bed.

"My son," Suri said through clenched teeth.

Leah rolled her eyes. Miriam kept her head turned away from Siri so the pregnant woman couldn't see the smile.

"Her waters broke just before you arrived," Leah said. She lifted the blanket, revealing Suri's lower body, and the cloths laid beneath her. "Tell me what you think."

Miriam looked at the thin legs, the swollen belly, and thought that whatever her age, the girl wasn't eating enough. Miriam knew better than to share that thought aloud. She ran her hand slowly over the distended belly, felt another contraction ripple through Suri's body. She ignored the child-woman's cries, the soothing words from Mylitta that followed, and floated her hands lower, feeling the baby move.

Miriam probed gently with her fingers the way the midwives had shown her when she helped them during the journey into Exile.

For one terrible, frightening moment, Miriam thought the baby was in the wrong position with its bottom ready to be born first. She took a long breath to calm her pounding heart, moved her hand again, probed once more, found what she expected.

Satisfied, Miriam wiped her hands on a cloth, looked at Leah, who had been watching her intently. "I don't think we have much longer to wait," she said.

Leah smiled. "Boy or girl, this one is impatient to be here, although for Suri's sake, I hope it is a boy. What disturbed you? I saw something on your face."

Miriam made sure her head was turned away from Suri. She spoke in a low voice so only Leah could hear. "I was afraid the baby was in the wrong position, bottom down, not head down."

"Be grateful it's head down," Leah said. A shadow seemed to flicker across her face, a flash of remembered sorrow in her hazel eyes. "I've only ever saved one child born that way, and we lost the mother. Pray you never experience it."

Miriam reached across, squeezed Leah's hand. "I'll pray you never have it happen again."

It was another three hours before the baby arrived and sesame oil lamps provided light as darkness fell.

An eternity for Suri, who wailed, cried, and screamed. She was exhausted when Leah finally cut the cord and handed the squalling infant to Miriam.

Miriam cradled the baby in her arms and gave thanks the child was indeed a boy. She wondered how it would feel to hold her own son, and what his name would be.

Jacob, possibly? It was another conversation she and Jacob needed to have.

Miriam wrapped the child in a cloth, murmured soothing words as he wailed and tried to fight the surrounding material.

Suri murmured a tired thank you as Miriam placed the baby on the new mother's breast. She winced as the tiny mouth fastened onto her nipple and began suckling.

"You'll get used to it sooner than you can believe," Mylitta said. "Do you have a name for him?"

"David," Suri said. "My husband says he will be named David. I hope he grows up to be more a psalmist than a warrior."

Suri stroked the cap of dark hair on the baby's head, giggled a little when he lifted his head and gave a soft belch, a dribble of milk running down his chin.

"He'll sleep now," Leah said. "And so should you. You'll need your strength for him."

She gestured to the couch and chairs on the far side of the room. "We won't be far. Call if you need anything," then to Miriam. "There's wine in the flagon on the table, and some fruit. Will you pour for us while I have the servants remove the soiled linens?"

Miriam felt the aches in the small of her back and in her thighs as she made her way across to the table and the wine. She had bent, crouched, and squatted throughout the labor, helping Leah as best she could.

She really, really wanted to spread herself on the couch and let her body rest, but Leah had done harder work.

Leah deserved the opportunity to lie back. Miriam turned away from the couch and took a chair facing the windows where lightning flickered, and thunder rumbled. It would be a good omen if the boy David brought relief from the heat, Miriam thought, as Mylitta sank into the chair opposite.

When the wine was poured, Leah had still not returned.

"Can I ask you something?" Miriam said to Mylitta after they'd both sipped from their wine.

"About Nurval?" There was a cautious tone in Mylitta's response.

"Partly," Miriam said. "I heard him say yesterday that, of course, Iddin was a thug. Why would he say that?"

Mylitta leaned forward to the platter of fruit. She touched the melon with her fingertips, frowned in distaste, then selected a pair of dates.

"Calling Iddin a thug wasn't meant unkindly," she said. "I asked Nurval how he knew he could trust Iddin, and that was his reply. Nurval grew up much the same in Haran and worked hard to leave that life behind, as Iddin is trying to do here."

"I understand it's a challenge for him," Miriam said. She picked up a piece of melon, felt the fruit soft under her fingers. Too soft, and she caught the too-sweet scent of it that told her the fruit was almost rotten. Miriam put the melon to one side and, like Mylitta, chose the dates.

"That's one reason Nurval decided to make the agreement with Iddin."

"What agreement?" Leah asked. She gave Miriam a quick smile of thanks, picked up her goblet of wine, and dropped onto the couch, lifting her legs and feet off the floor with a long sigh of relief. And then another sigh as she took a long swallow of wine.

"I hope Suri and the baby will sleep long and hard, but experience tells me it's unlikely. Now tell me, what agreement?"

"Nurval was making little progress in negotiations with the temple of Marduk. He wanted someone he trusted to continue after we returned to Haran. Iddin was that person, so I don't understand why Iddin would send one of his men to kill Nurval."

"He was Iddin's man?" Miriam nearly spilled her wine. She hoped Jacob knew this before his visit to see Iddin. Likely, they had already met. She offered a prayer the meeting had not gone badly.

Mylitta was nodding, the movement endangering her own wine. "So the priest, Arioch, and his guard said."

Praise be, Miriam thought. At least Jacob had a warning.

"Why would Arioch come here if he was being so difficult with his negotiations?" Leah asked.

Mylitta shook her head. "Nurval wasn't dealing with Arioch. It was something to do with the sheep herds. All he told me was it would give the temple of Marduk control over our herds in Haran. That wasn't acceptable."

"Why kill your husband?" Miriam asked.

"His brother. He inherits everything and will agree to anything if there is immediate money in his hand. He has no vision for the future."

Mylitta's tone told Miriam everything.

Something more to tell Jacob, Miriam thought. She sighed as Suri cried out, her voice sharp with pain. Miriam reached for her bag with the pain remedies as Leah swung her feet to the floor.

CHAPTER NINETEEN

The eighth day of Abu - Evening

It was evening before Jacob made his way across the city of Babylon to Enlil Street, and to the Te-Eki ward. He had spoken with Isaac, then returned home and changed into an older robe that had patches on the sleeves and stains down the front. In the half-dark, he doubted anyone would notice the stains. If he added more stains, it wouldn't matter.

Outwardly, he appeared unarmed, but he had followed up on his thought at Iddin's house earlier in the day, strapped a small knife to the inside of his right forearm, and a second on the inside of his left calf.

It had taken him most of the afternoon to persuade Ligish not to join him. In one respect, Jacob would have welcomed the company, and someone he trusted to watch his back. Even in rags, Ligish could not hide that he walked and moved like a soldier. If he joined Jacob, they would achieve nothing, and probably attract some very unwelcome attention.

Evening had turned Enlil street from a busy thoroughfare, bringing goods and pilgrims into Babylon from the south, to an eerie, and almost empty street.

There were no lamps on Enlil Street like there were on Marduk Street and Processional Way, the major thoroughfares of the city.

Te-Eki was one of the older wards in the city. The New Town ward in the north-east of the city, where Jacob lived, was all houses with an occasional building that allowed several families to live together in a community. Te-Eki was a haphazard mix of homes, workshops, and warehouses, some buildings being all three.

Here in Te-Eki, Jacob walked between pools of yellow light thrown out by the inns, taverns, and other places he assumed were brothels or gambling houses. The chatter of noise, the notes of lyres and flutes, a crash of furniture and raised voices, came to him as he passed each place.

The sour aroma of refuse drifted around Jacob and mingled with the smells of cooking and sesame oil. It was a strange combination, but mostly the food won. Jacob's stomach growled, reminding him he'd eaten nothing since the snacks Iddin offered earlier in the day.

Jacob doubted he would eat much tonight, either. He needed his wits about him, not the warm drowsy feeling that came after a good meal, and a glass or two of wine.

Iddin's information was slightly inaccurate. There were no inns or taverns where Enlil Street met Zababa Street.

Jacob kept walking toward the Enlil Gate, knowing it was a dead end at this time of day. The gate was closed until sunrise; the guards had returned to their barracks. There were a few other people on the street, traveling in both directions. No-one seemed to pay him any special attention.

Jacob let out a small sigh of relief when he heard the noise of an inexpertly played lyre, the notes coming out harshly rather than the soft, tender sound Jacob was used to hearing.

Others must have agreed with his thoughts.

As Jacob reached the entrance to the tavern, there were harsh shouts and hard words, and the lyre fell silent to a chorus of appreciation.

It was perhaps not the best time to enter the tavern. With no entertainment to occupy them, the customers turned and watched as Jacob entered, their conversation fading away.

Jacob made his way toward the elderly woman stirring the contents of a vat, whose width was the size of Jacob's outstretched arms.

The looks from the customers, as he weaved between the tables, were guarded and suspicious, openly hostile in some cases.

This was a tavern where the customers were local. Likely, everyone lived within three or four streets. They knew each other, worked together, partied and fought together, and were wary of strangers.

It was also a tavern where you didn't ask for wine.

For these people, wine was a luxury item they couldn't afford. Jacob handed over some coppers. The woman inspected the coins in the light of a nearby sesame oil lamp, pushed them into a pocket and dipped a mug into the vat.

She handed the mug to Jacob with a drinking tube to strain out any solids. One careful mouthful told Jacob what he suspected. This was a beer made with cheap barley, possibly the leavings on the mill floor, and normal for a tavern like this.

Jacob eased himself between more patrons, careful not to knock their arms or spill their drinks. He looked around him as he moved, giving the impression of looking for someone. When he appeared unable to find the person he searched for, Jacob selected a small table at the back of the room. The three-legged stool was unstable and rocked and creaked as he put his weight on it.

When he was settled, Jacob leaned back against the wall so he could see the door and most of the customers.

Around Jacob, the conversations slowly started again. The voices were low and too far away for Jacob to hear what was being said, but he caught the cadence and tone of what was being said, and the accents of the speakers.

It was the accents that surprised him.

Iddin had said Judeans weren't welcome here, yet he was sure he heard the distinctive accents of Jerusalem and Hebron mixed with the harsher tones of Babylon.

Had Iddin sent him into a trap?

A movement on his right shoulder brought Jacob out of his musings. Two men stood before the table. In the dim light, with most of the lamps behind them, Jacob could see little more than two silhouettes, both taller than him, and both wider by a considerable amount.

"Haven't seen you here before," said the man on the right, the one closest to Jacob.

He wasn't Babylonian. Jacob didn't think he was Judean either.

"My first time," Jacob said. "I'm hoping to meet someone, but I'm thinking he won't be here tonight."

"We know all the people who come here. Give us his name, and I can tell you when he's usually here."

Jacob placed the mug of beer on the table. He folded his arms in front of the mug, let his left hand slide inside the sleeve of his robe, right beside the hilt of the knife strapped to his forearm. He felt confident he could deal with the man before him. Not so confident he could handle both of them, and get out of the tavern without some bruises.

For a moment, Jacob considered abandoning the search for information about Sadudu and asking about Asher. Then he discarded the thought. He had a story prepared for Sadudu, nothing but guesswork for Asher, and that could get him into trouble.

"I'm looking for Sadudu," he said. "I have some work that would suit his talents."

"Then you're lucky to have found me," the first man said.

Jacob allowed himself a smile, grateful for the detailed description Miriam had given him.

"A good try, my friend. Your beard is too long, and if you are Sadudu, you've grown a head or more in height since you left Iddin's employ."

The two exchanged a look that in the half-light that Jacob couldn't interpret. It seemed neither man knew Sadudu was dead. It didn't surprise Jacob that the information hadn't reached Te-Eki, but he still wasn't sure how to turn it to his advantage.

"Worth a try," the first man said with a smile. "We haven't seen Sadudu in four or five days. He keeps his own counsel about his movements, so it might be another four or five days before we see him again. What is it you need him for? We might not have all his skills, but there are two of us."

Jacob took a sip of the beer. It didn't taste any better, but it gave him a few seconds to decide how far to go with these two.

"Two might be an advantage," he said. "If you're interested."

"We might," the first one said. "It's not something we'd do for free though, seeing as we don't really know who you are."

"I wouldn't expect it, but I'm sure we can come to an agreement," Jacob said.

Another glance between the two, and a slight nod of agreement Jacob would have missed if he hadn't been looking for and expecting it.

"Not here," the second one said. "Follow us."

Jacob relaxed a little, felt a surge of anticipation that he'd maybe crossed the path Asher had followed. He carried a few coins with him, knew those he had wouldn't be enough to satisfy these two.

It meant another meeting, but he accepted that. Gideon had taught him that sometimes it wasn't possible to achieve everything on one mission.

And hadn't that been a hard lesson to learn?

Jacob left the mug, still half-full, on the table, like he would come back. He knew the half of the beer he'd drunk would likely churn and curdle in his stomach. Already, he felt the soft cramps and churning in his gut.

That was a problem for the morning, he decided, and pushed to his feet. He followed the first man, aware of the second behind, crowding him a little on the right-hand side. All the better if they thought he was right-handed.

As they reached the doorway, the man behind dropped back a step. Jacob switched his attention to the man in front, expecting him to turn, make some movement.

A blur to his right.

Jacob got his arm up, barely in time.

The fist hit him just above the right elbow. The same place the Babylonian sword had slashed him all those years ago.

Jacob cried out, stumbled back, had no defense when the second blow landed in his stomach.

There was no keeping the beer down now.

Jacob felt the bile rush into his throat. He didn't try to stop it, jerked his head to the left so the stream of vomit hit the third man in the face as he came in for another blow.

A string of curses, and Jacob saw a chance.

He stumbled left, the pain in his arm almost blinding. He reached inside his right sleeve, fumbled for the knife. His fingers tangled.

Just as he got a solid grip, something thudded into his shoulder. Jacob tumbled away, his balance gone. He hit the ground, rolled, winced as the weight came onto his right arm. Rolled once more, felt a rough mud-brick wall scrape his back.

His arms and legs were twisted. Everything was in the wrong place, and at the wrong angle for him to get easily to his feet.

The attackers knew this and pressed their advantage.

Jacob got his right arm up to protect his head, but there was no relief for his body, or his right thigh, which was numb from the continual pounding.

"Enough!" the first man said, his voice breathless.

Jacob heard movement. The scuff of feet on the packed earth of the street. Two pairs of hands grabbed his shoulders, dragged him upright, slammed him back against the wall.

Jacob winced as the rough edges of the bricks scored his back. The force of the shove banged his head against the wall. His vision darkened into a long, narrow tunnel.

There was a point of light a long, long way away. He focused on the pinpoint, afraid that if he let it go, he would never wake again.

Slowly, the point of light grew, became the wash of dirty yellow light coming from the tavern, partly obscured by the bulk of the first man.

"You're going to answer some questions," he said. "Just understand you have no choice. We can keep this up all night and drop what's left of you in the river after the Enlil Street gate opens at dawn. Why are you looking for Sadudu?"

"I told you. I have some work for him."

Jacob was about to add to the offer when the third man cuffed him. His head hit the wall and for a moment, everything went gray.

"There's a problem with that," the first man said. "You see, Sadudu died at the Summer Palace yesterday afternoon. I was told a Judean woman had a lot to do with that. And now here are you, another Judean asking questions."

"What do we do with him? The caravans?" the second man asked before Jacob could say anything.

"There's too much going on there," the first man said. There was a breathless excitement in his next words. "I doubt he knows where the woman went. Let's get him into the warehouse by the gate. We can ask him those questions and teach him some lessons. After that, we'll drop what's left into the river."

"I like that idea," the third man said.

Jacob sensed the man move, had no time to avoid the fist that drove into his stomach taking the wind from him. As Jacob doubled over, there was another blow to the side of his head and he was falling.

The pinpoint of light was there again, bright, white, and beckoning. Jacob tried to hold on to it. He tried to bring it closer, but he had nothing left, no energy.

The light faded away into the darkness.

CHAPTER TWENTY

The ninth day of Abu - Morning

Miriam came awake before dawn with a sick, nauseous feeling in her stomach. An escort of Palace Guards had brought her through the Marduk Gate after sundown. Even then, she had slept badly.

She pushed the light blanket off her body, lay still on the straw pallet. In her head, Miriam counted the days, reassured herself her courses really had finished, and decided she had either slept awkwardly, or something in last night's meal disagreed with her.

She rolled over to look at the balcony doorway she had left uncovered the previous evening. Her hope was there would be some wind that blew cooler air into the room. The fabric of the door coverings remained still, the air dry and hot, a soft light coming into the room from the half-moon she could see through the doorway.

Miriam let out a long sigh. If the weather didn't change in another day or so, she would be dealing with heat sickness amongst the older people, and the very, very young, like Suri's new son, David.

She didn't believe the heat caused her nausea, though. Heat like this was common in the middle of Babylon's summers. Miriam didn't like these summers, but after all the years in Babylon, she was used to them now.

Still restless, she rolled again, the straw mattress crackling as she moved her weight and shifted to a sitting position. Her sleeping shift was damp with perspiration. She pulled it over her head, wiped her body, reached over for her robe and slipped that on.

There was a gentle movement of air on the balcony that was so slight, Miriam thought she imagined it when she first stepped outside. The movement wasn't enough to cool anything, but it was a pleasant respite from the heavy stillness that had covered Babylon for the past days.

She settled into the chair beside the door, easing down onto the seat so it didn't creak and disturb anyone else in the house. The night time chatter of the cicadas was muted. Miriam estimated it was maybe an hour before dawn, and the wood smoke she smelled was servants in nearby houses, preparing early meals for their masters.

It wouldn't be long before Isaac's servants began their morning routine. Like a comment on her thought, Solly shuffled across the courtyard below her, heading toward the street door.

Miriam took a series of long breaths, taking air in, then letting it out slowly and evenly. The breathing helped the discomfort in her stomach and she turned her attention back to Solly, who had reached the door and peered out into the street.

Solly was little more than a shadow, but Miriam was certain something alarmed him from the way his body tensed.

Then he disappeared.

Miriam came to her feet when she saw Solly reappear. He half-carried, half-dragged something through the door.

Solly looked up, his face a pale blur as he looked around desperately for help. He saw her and his voice was high, reedy, and panicked.

"Miriam. Help!"

And now Miriam knew the reason for her nausea.

Her bare feet pounded along the balcony walkway. She didn't care about the noise now, nearly missed the top step, adjusted her stride and almost fell down the stairs. She stumbled at the bottom, grabbed the handrail to balance herself.

Solly had fallen to his knees under the weight on his shoulders. It became more than he could bear, and he leaned to his right.

Miriam reached Solly before he completely lost his balance.

She hooked her hands under Jacob's shoulders. She was certain the heavy, unresponsive body was Jacob. Her hands skidded on something slippery. Blood or vomit.

Both, judging by the smell.

She hooked her hands again, getting her forearms under Jacob's shoulders. Miriam grunted as his full weight came on her. She nearly fell, dug her heels into the packed earth, strained a little, then carefully slid Jacob off Solly and onto his back.

"Get the servants, and water, and cloths," Miriam said to Solly. "We'll put him on one of the couches, and see. And see . . ."

She couldn't finish the thought.

"Jacob's a mess, but he's alive. He spoke to me," Solly said. He put a comforting hand on her shoulder, then hurried away to the servant's rooms.

Miriam moved, so the moonlight shone directly on Jacob. Solly was right. He was a mess.

For a moment, she feared she would be ill.

You saw worse on the trek into Exile; she scolded herself.

And she had, but those injuries were to men and women who meant nothing to her.

This was Jacob.

The servants came reluctantly, cajoled and harangued by Solly. Four of them. Miriam positioned two on each side while she held Jacob's head. They lifted him carefully and moved slowly across the courtyard to one of the long couches.

Jacob's body twisted as they laid him on the couch. He cried out, then groaned, and sobbed before subsiding, moving so his right arm was uppermost. His arm flopped, falling over the side of the couch like he had no control of it.

Miriam turned away, afraid they would see the tears that blurred her vision.

"Watch him," she said to Solly, and ran for the steps. She needed the herbs and salves from her room.

At the top of the stairs, she ran into something solid and nearly fell.

It was becoming a habit; she thought as hands gripped her upper arms and held her upright.

"What is going on?" Isaac demanded. He wore sleeping trews and nothing else, the half-light showing the tousled hair plastered across his head.

"Jacob," Miriam said. "Solly found him on the street outside the door. He's hurt."

Once, he would have lectured her.

"I'll get Esther," he said, and turned back to his bedroom.

Miriam went past him, back to her own room. She pulled the chest from under her bed, opened it.

She worked from memory in the dim light, selected four small jars, then a fifth, and hurried back outside.

The servants had placed a large jug, a bowl, and a pile of rags on the table beside the couch. They stood in an arc, uncertain what to do next, until Esther's sharp voice cut across the silence.

"Bring lamps as well, enough to see what we are doing," she said, then in a gentler voice to Miriam. "How bad?"

Miriam shook her head. "If you help me, we'll find out."

And then she realized how the light had changed as dawn came.

"What about Shema?"

"Today, He will understand if we focus on healing Jacob," Esther said. "What do you want me to do?"

Missing Shema still felt wrong, but Miriam knew that was because of the habits drilled into her from a young age by her father, the priest, and then her husband. She took a long breath, deciding she would pray later in the day, then forced her attention to shift back to Jacob.

The early morning light revealed Jacob's injuries more clearly to her.

There was blood matted in Jacob's hair, in his beard, and smeared across his face. His eyes were closed, and there was a tightness around his mouth that told her he was in pain. The robe was ruined, and Miriam she was relieved to see it was an older garment Jacob probably used for dirty jobs. It was probably well suited for his visit to Te-Eki.

"We need to cut the robe off him, and see if there are other injuries," she said to Esther. "We'll cut it up the front, then along the sleeves, and be very careful with his right arm. I don't like the way he seems to have no use of it."

Esther hurried to get a knife from the kitchen.

Miriam squatted beside Jacob, her face level with his head. She reached for his left hand, curled hers round his fingers, felt the scrapes and abrasion on his knuckles, and kept her grip loose.

"Jacob, we're going to cut your robe away so I can make sure you've no injuries elsewhere."

"No need," he said in a hoarse whisper. "Give me an hour or two. I have to see Ligish."

"You're going nowhere," she said.

Miriam released his hand and placed hers on his chest, holding him down as he struggled to sit up.

It was a brief struggle. Jacob winced as the pain hit him. He dropped back onto the couch.

"Lie still," she said.

"I'll have Isaac send Solly for Ligish. You can tell the story to us all once we have you cleaned up."

"That I would rather not do," he said with an attempt at a smile. A smile that turned into a cough, making him wince.

Miriam watched the spittle that came from his mouth as he coughed. The spittle was clear with no signs of a pink stain or a bloody foam. She felt some of her tension ease. At least he didn't appear to have damaged something inside him. Something she could not fix.

"I brought two knives," Esther said, coming up beside Miriam and offering her a bronze hilt.

Miriam took the knife. As Esther began cutting through Jacob's robe from the bottom, Miriam used the knife and began cutting from the neckline toward his right shoulder.

"You will be careful with that, won't you?" Jacob said.

Miriam answered almost before Jacob had finished speaking. "As long as you lay still and do as you're told."

She spoke more sharply than she intended, felt a twinge of guilt, and glanced at him. There was a small smile on his face as his half-open eyes watched her work.

"I think you'll be the one who enforces discipline on our children," he said.

"If they are as wild as either of you, I doubt anyone will control them," Esther said, and there was laughter in her voice that robbed the words of any sting.

"Likely," Miriam admitted, then frowned as she cut away the right sleeve of Jacob's robe.

She gestured at the binding on Jacob's forearm. "What's this?"

This time, he smiled without a wince. "An idea I borrowed from you, so I had a weapon with me. There's another on my leg."

"I wondered what that was," Esther said. "At least it's not another wound we have to treat."

Miriam studied the bruises, scrapes, and oozing blood on Jacob's right arm. They clustered round the livid, ridged scar just above his elbow. She suspected the weakness he was showing was the bruising and not a sign of something deeper and more crippling.

"Where are the knives?" Miriam asked, working to keep her voice level.

"I left them behind."

His tone warned Miriam not to ask more. At least not yet.

She moved aside as Esther finished slicing the front of the robe. Working together, they rolled the robe off Jacob's body, revealing more scrapes and bruises.

"We're going to clean up your cuts and scrapes," Miriam said. "After that, there's a salve for your bruises, and then you can eat."

"Have someone watch me," Jacob said. "Don't let me fall asleep, or if I do, wake me, no matter how surly I am."

"Why?" Miriam asked.

"I was hit on the head," he said. "I had strange things happen to my soldiers who were hit on the head, even when they wore a helmet. Watch me for signs of drowsiness, and keep me awake as long as possible."

"How many times were you hit on the head?" Miriam asked.

"A few."

Miriam sensed he wasn't being fully honest with her. Either he didn't want her to know, or he really didn't know himself. She wasn't sure which disturbed her the most and decided not to push Jacob too hard.

She was certain with help from Esther and Solly, they could watch him.

"I'll make sure someone is with you all day," she said. "Now lie still and let us clean you up."

It took over an hour, with Esther's help, to clean the dried and crusted blood from Jacob's body, bind up the worst of the cuts, and apply salve to the bruises beginning to blossom into a rainbow of reds, purples, and yellows.

When they were done, the sun was high above the walls of the house. The breath of coolness Miriam had felt before the dawn was gone. Jacob shivered like a man having a fever. Despite his protests, Miriam covered him with a heavy blanket and fed him with the fruit the servants brought for breakfast.

It was late morning before Ligish arrived. Miriam thought he looked tired, haggard, almost, and forgave the sharpness of his tone.

"What happened?"

"I don't know," she said. "It seemed best to wait for you, so Jacob tells the story once. The servants are bringing wine and fruit."

Ligish nodded, ran a hand through his dark hair, and the look on his face changed. "If I thought this would happen, I would never have let him go alone."

"He worried about your safety," Miriam said.

"And ignores his own," Ligish said. "I think I will need that wine you mentioned."

The servants had placed wine and fruit on the table. Miriam directed Ligish to a chair. When Ligish was settled, and after the wine was blessed and poured, Miriam turned to Jacob. He had shrugged off the blanket and swung his legs to the ground so she could sit beside him on the couch.

"I think it's time you told us what happened," she said.

"A lot of stiff-necked arrogance," Jacob said with a smile that didn't quite reach his brown eyes.

"I assumed I knew more than anyone I would meet in Te-Eki, and that I could talk my way out of any situation."

"Iddin warned us they don't like Judeans in Te-Eki," Ligish said.

"He did."

Jacob took a sip of the wine, grimaced at the taste, and put the goblet back on the table.

"What Iddin didn't tell us," Jacob said, leaning back on the couch. "There are many Judeans in Te-Eki. I saw and heard them in the tavern near the Elli Gate. They ignored me, especially after Sadudu's companions approached me."

"What does that mean?" Miriam asked.

"Probably nothing," Jacob said. "I'd like to know why Iddin lied to us. It may just be mischief on his part, but I don't think it will help us find Asher's killers."

"What can the men who approached you tell us?" Ligish asked.

"Nothing now," Jacob said.

Ligish raised an eyebrow, and Jacob continued. "They decided I wasn't worth taking to their caravan and planned to throw me in the river when the Enlil Gate opened. It was my good fortune they didn't consider me worth searching for a weapon."

Miriam shivered despite the heat, suddenly aware of how close she had come to losing Jacob. She kept her hands folded in her lap so neither man would see them shaking. Ligish had begun talking, and she forced herself to focus on his words.

"So we're no closer to finding out who killed Asher, and who is behind the campaign against Arioch."

"Perhaps we are," Miriam said, remembering the things she had learned at the Summer Palace. "According to his wife, Mylitta, Nurval was being pressured to make an agreement that would have placed all his herds, here and in Haran, effectively under the control of the temple of Marduk. Now he's dead, his brother controls everything."

She saw Jacob look at Ligish. "What do you know of the brother?"

"Nothing good," Ligish said, confirming the impression Miriam had formed when she spoke with Mylitta. "Arioch wasn't working with Nurval, but I can find out who was."

He pushed to his feet when Miriam said. "There's one more thing, although I don't know if it means anything."

Quickly she told them about Ruth, and her impression of the woman's fear.

"It's too much of a coincidence. We should talk to her," Jacob said.

He made to stand. His face paled, and he drew in a sharp breath. Miriam put her hand on his chest and pushed him back into the couch cushions.

"You are going nowhere today. If you seem better tomorrow, then we can visit Ruth."

CHAPTER TWENTY-ONE

The tenth day of Abu - Afternoon

Although he was reluctant to admit it, the day of rest Miriam insisted on had worked better than Jacob expected. He still ached in more places than he cared to count, and the bruises, especially on his right arm, had blossomed into brown, yellow, red, and purple colors.

The walk from Isaac's house to the village of Kweiresh helped as well. Jacob had begun the journey slowly. As the movement through the streets stretched his muscles, the really painful aches disappeared. Jacob moved more freely, at first able to keep up with Miriam's long paces, then able to match them. He didn't think he could run yet, and decided to save that energy for the next day, or maybe the day after.

It wasn't the first time he'd been alone with Miriam, but though it was two months since Isaac and Esther had decided a chaperone wasn't needed for the, it still felt a little strange, and Jacob kept wanting to turn and look for Solly.

They followed the road from the Sin Gate and entered Kweiresh from the southeast, weaving through a maze of streets until they reach a crossroads, where Miriam paused.

"This is the place." Miriam said, then pointed. "The house on the right side of the alleyway is Ruth's. The one on the left is the inn with the brewery."

A cart laden with vegetables rumbled, trailing the aroma of onions. Jacob noted it, the people walking back and forth as he studied the buildings Miriam pointed out.

Ruth's home was three stories of tan colored mud bricks. There was none of the decoration to break up the glare of the sun, like there was on most houses inside the city walls.

Jacob noted one entrance on the street where he stood with Miriam, and narrow windows on the floors above. The side of the house facing the alleyway had no doors or windows.

The inn, which was a generous name for the building, was two stories of mud brick. The corners of the bricks had crumbled, leaving ragged, uneven edges along the walls, and added to the air of neglect. Three doorways ran along the alley side of the building, each covered with dirty and stained cloth rather than the expected animal hide.

Jacob suspected the inn struggled to make enough money to remain in business, or the owner spent as little as possible. Likely, it was some of both. Jacob suspected the only reason Gideon's inn appeared so successful was because of the gold and silver he earned from his information gathering.

"I can smell the brewery," Jacob said. He resisted the impulse to put a hand over his face and shield his nose from the sour odor that came from the alley. He could almost taste it, which wasn't good. The taste was sour and cheap barley beer, like the brew he had drunk in Te-Eki two nights before.

"Ruth said the girl came out of the inn, turned left, fought off an attacker, and ran away?"

"That's right," Miriam said.

Jacob studied the alleyway, the buildings on both sides, the refuse strewn across the packed earth, the wall at the far end about twice his height.

"There's no way out of the alley if the girl turned left out of the inn," Jacob said. "It's a dead end."

"I knew something felt wrong when I looked out into the alley," Miriam said with a sigh of frustration. "What else did I miss?"

"Likely nothing," Jacob said. "You found the cloak brooch," Jacob said, then after a pause to collect his thoughts.

"Ruth told you she would never go into the place and then told you she doubted Simon had replaced the door to the room."

"That's right," Miriam said.

Jacob saw the slight widening of her eyes as she realized what he meant. "How did she know about the door?"

"Let's ask her," Jacob said, and started across the street.

"Jacob, wait."

Her hand gripped the sleeve of his robe, not quite pulling him back, but not ready to let him move freely.

Jacob stopped, waited as she stepped round so they were face-to-face, her hand still on his sleeve.

"I met Ruth during the journey into Exile."

She broke off like she didn't know what to say next. Or maybe how to say it, Jacob realized.

He took her hand from his sleeve, held it in his own, distracted for a moment by her warmth and closeness.

"You know, Ruth, and you should talk to her," he said. "I'll stay out of the way as much as I can."

He saw her throat move as she swallowed hard.

"Thank you," she said, and moved her hand away, leaving him feeling a sense of loss.

They crossed the street side-by-side. Miriam pushed aside the ox-hide door covering and led the way into the herb shop.

Jacob paused just inside the hide covering, letting Miriam go forward alone. There were rows and rows of herbs hanging on strips of papyrus or hooks, and in layers from knee height almost to the ceiling. Some were fresh. Others dried.

The scent of rosemary almost overwhelmed him, a welcome change from the stink of bad beer that hung over the street.

As he looked round, Jacob realized he needed to rethink the plan for Miriam's herb room at the house. The size he had built was good, but the inside needed at least twice as much space for drying herbs. He saw an iron brazier in the far corner of the room. The brazier was cold, with gray ash and half-burned coals in the bottom.

Miriam hadn't asked for a brazier, but Jacob saw how it would be useful for her as she made salves and tonics. He recognized many of the herbs as well, especially the rosemary and lavender. With the right combination of soil and water, both should grow well at the house.

Jacob returned his attention to the room, noting the heavy blanket that covered a doorway and, he assumed, led to the rest of the house. He heard movement and the sound of feet on a staircase.

The blanket shifted. He heard the thud as something was put down, then a pudgy hand pulled the blanket aside and a short, heavyset woman with a ruddy face came into the room.

Jacob guessed this was Ruth.

Ruth smiled when she saw Miriam, realized Jacob was there, and her face closed up. The fear Miriam had described sparked in Ruth's dark eyes.

"Miriam. This is a surprise. What brings you back so quickly? I hope you're not looking for more tarkhun. I sold the last yesterday. It will be at least seven or ten days before I get more. What is it you're looking for?"

Her voice was bright. Too bright, pitched a little high, the words coming out too fast.

Definitely scared, Jacob thought. He watched her eyes dart from Miriam to himself, and back again.

Letting Miriam talk had been the right decision.

"Not the tarkhun," Miriam said, apparently ignoring the woman's discomfort. "I need more yarrow, Ruth. Jacob here got himself into a situation and I used everything I had on his bruises."

For the first time, Ruth looked at Jacob properly, saw the scrapes and bruises on his face.

She shook her head and said. "Some situation. I have two bunches of fresh, and I can let you have five shekels of dried. I have my own."

Ruth stopped abruptly, and Jacob saw her face flush even redder.

"You have bruises?" Miriam asked. "Where are you hurt? Can I help?"

Jacob admired the way Miriam reacted so quickly to the other woman's words.

"Not me," Ruth said quickly. Her eyes flickered from Miriam to

Jacob as they had before, and her voice was flustered. "I meant my other customers. The other people who buy my herbs."

"What about the woman from the inn?" Jacob asked, keeping his voice soft and neutral, taking a chance. "You couldn't have seen her from the window, Ruth. There isn't one. And she couldn't run the way you told Miriam she did. The wall at the end of the alley would have trapped her. Do you know where she is?"

Ruth stepped back, standing in front of the blanket. She shook her head from side to side. Her whole body shook with fear. Jacob saw the bright sheen of unshed tears in her eyes.

"We are here to help you," he said, and took another chance. "Asher was one of my oldest friends."

There was a noise of movement and a shuffle of feet from elsewhere in the house. Jacob wasn't wearing a sword, hadn't thought to bring a knife or a dagger with him. Most of the hooks were carved from wood, but at the end furthest from the door, he saw the shine of bronze or, hopefully, iron.

Jacob took a slow breath. He tensed his muscles, ignored the pain from the bruises as he prepared for the rush across the room to free a hook and use it as a weapon.

"It's all right, Ruth," a woman said as she pushed through the blanket and into the shop. She laid a reassuring hand on Ruth's shoulder and looked from Miriam to Jacob. "Asher said you would eventually find me. I am Debra."

Jacob exchanged a long look with Miriam. She looked as stunned and confused as he felt. If this woman was the Debra Asher asked him to find and protect, who was the woman with Sibri?

CHAPTER TWENTY-TWO

The tenth day of Abu - Afternoon

Miriam looked away from the surprised expression on Jacob's face and focused on the woman standing beside Ruth.

Debra was about Miriam's height, with hair as dark as a moonless night that cascading down over her shoulders almost to her elbows. Her face was round, but not chubby. There were fine lines around her dark eyes and she had full lips that seemed about to smile despite the air of grief she carried.

She looked maybe five years older than Miriam, and that surprised Miriam. She understood Asher to be several years younger than Jacob.

Asher and this Debra seemed an odd match, but she had obviously cared very much about him.

"I believe we have something that belongs to you," Miriam said, looking for an indirect way to have Debra tell her story.

"My brooch? Praise be," Debra's face lit up, and it was like a different woman was revealed. "Thank you. It was a gift from my husband. I feared it was lost."

Husband!

Miriam almost laughed at the look on Jacob's face, although she was sure her expression mirrored his.

His voice sounded equally confused. "What. . . How did you know Asher?"

This time, Debra's smile was sad and wistful. "I appreciate the care with which you ask a hard question. Asher and my husband worked together."

It still made little sense to Miriam, so she said. "I think it would help to start from the beginning?"

"Let me get wine," Ruth said. "And stools. Both will help with the telling of this story."

When the wine was blessed and poured, and they were settled on the stools, Debra, who sat opposite Miriam, pushed a hand through her hair, and Miriam saw strands of gray threading through the black.

"My husband was a scribe for the Temple in Jerusalem. He was rarely there, always out in the fields with the shepherds and goat herders. After Jerusalem fell, the Babylonians pressed him to work for the temple here, and we settled in Borsippa."

She took a sip of the wine, and nearly spilled it when there was a noise from the street.

A figure appeared in the doorway.

Ruth sprang to her feet. "Customers," she said as she moved to the door.

From the corner of her eye, Miriam saw Jacob settle back onto his stool, his hand moving away from the metal hook that held several bunches of rosemary.

He sensed her watching him, gave a shrug that might have been an apology, or might have just said, you know this is who I am.

Miriam smiled back at him. Couldn't help herself.

Debra said. "How long have you been married?"

Miriam felt the color flush her cheeks. "We are betrothed but not yet married. There is a caravan returning from Judah with people who should be at our wedding. That is when we will marry."

As she said the words, Miriam vowed to herself that whatever obstacles Isaac, or anyone else, put in their way, she would marry Jacob on the Sabbath after the return of the Judah caravan.

Miriam shook herself out of her thoughts when she heard Ruth call her name.

"Miriam. If I let you have three bunches of fresh yarrow, can you leave the dried for another seven days?"

Miriam pretended to consider the offer. She had plenty of yarrow at Isaac's house, despite the injuries to Jacob, and the request had been to get Ruth talking. She nodded.

"I can do that, and I'll make sure Jacob gets no more bruises."

"Little chance of that, I think," Ruth said with a laugh that conveyed her gratitude.

When the customers had their herbs and left, Debra returned to her story.

"I liked Asher," she said. "I'm sure you know he was working for the temple of Marduk here in Babylon. He seemed awkward and embarrassed to ask for help."

"What was he looking for?" Jacob asked, an instant before Miriam opened her mouth to ask the same question.

Debra switched her look between the two of them, like once more she had seen more than she said.

"Asher wanted to understand how the herd management worked and who reported to who in the temple. Not just the shepherds to the overseers to the priests, but who really makes the decisions."

"Isn't that Subisha?" Jacob asked.

There was something in the way he asked the question that made Miriam think this was a test.

Miriam watched Debra closely, and if the other woman sensed the test, she showed no sign of it.

"You would think so," Debra said. "What I understood from the conversation between Asher and my husband is that Subisha is a figurehead. Someone else in the temple is really controlling the management of the herds. Whoever they are is seeking more control and becoming ruthless toward anyone who may be an obstacle."

"Do you know who?" Miriam asked.

"If I did, they would be dead," Debra said in a bitter voice. "They killed my husband, and my guess is they killed Asher as well. Asher saved me when men came to our house. They had no interest in asking questions. They were there to kill." She jerked her head toward the wall. "He thought we were safe at the inn."

Then she turned the original question back to Miriam and Jacob. "Do you know who?"

"I have some ideas," Jacob said. "I am not certain enough at the moment to give you a name. Whoever it is, I owe them for Asher. And now your husband."

Jacob had been leaning forward, elbows on his knees. As he straightened and flexed his back, Miriam saw the flicker of pain ripple across his face. The look was gone quickly, and there was no trace of it when he looked at Miriam.

"We need to talk to the person with Sibri," he said. "And quickly."

Miriam shifted her attention to Ruth and Debra. "Can Debra stay with you for another day or two, Ruth? There are many Judeans here in Kweiresh, and in Babylon who will help you, Debra, but we must make it safe for you first."

"You're welcome to stay with me as long as you wish," Ruth said to Debra.

For the first time, Miriam saw the grief and sense of loss overwhelm Debra. Her head went down, and her shoulders shook.

As Ruth moved to comfort Debra, Miriam reached over and snagged Jacob's sleeve. This was their excuse to leave.

"You forgot the yarrow," Jacob said as they made their way out of Kweiresh and onto the road that ran beside the irrigation canal and led to the caravan grounds.

"Ruth knows herbs weren't the real reason for our visit," Miriam said, then voiced the question that had worried at her since they first saw Debra.

"What are we going to do about the other Debra?"

"Get some answers," Jacob said, and there was a hard edge to his voice she'd never heard before.

The sound of it scared her a little, and they walked in silence for several minutes before Miriam said.

"Let me talk to her first. She might be more open with me."

For a long time Jacob didn't respond, and Miriam was certain he was going to refuse her when finally, he said.

"That makes sense. I'm not sure I have the patience to ease answers from her. We're still not sure how involved she was with Asher's death, so I will be very close."

"That also makes sense," Miriam said, and was pleased to see Jacob smile at her repetition of his words.

The rest of the journey was in companionable silence without the tension that had been there when they left Ruth's shop.

"Sibri's not happy," Jacob said as they reached the caravan grounds.

Miriam gave up wiping the dust from her face, followed where Jacob was looking, and saw Sibri coming toward them with a fast limp. He winced every time the injured leg, the one a mule had rolled on, hit the ground, and there was worry and concern on his sharp angular face.

"What's wrong?" Jacob asked, reaching a hand out to steady Sibri as the man reached them, his breath wheezing in and out. "The girl, Debra. Is she all right?"

"Take your time," Miriam said. "Get your breath back first."

Sibri gave her a grateful smile and heaved in two more long breaths.

"If you mean, is she hurt, then no," he said. "What she is, is scared, Jacob. She won't leave the room unless it's dark. Even then, she keeps looking around like she expects someone to jump out and steal her away."

"Is she eating?" Miriam asked.

Sibri shrugged. "She accepts food, but I think the rats are eating more than she does."

"Your idea of talking with her was a good one." Jacob said. He glanced at the sun sinking into the western sky.

"Let's do it now. I'll wait on the stairs outside the door. Call for me if anything doesn't feel right. I won't risk you getting hurt."

Miriam nodded. She agreed it was better to get this over with now, and find out who this Debra really was. And she couldn't argue with his desire to protect her.

In truth, she was nervous about facing the woman alone. Miriam straightened her back, pushed her shoulders back, and crossed the last paces on the dusty earth to the building.

The mud brick stairs felt slippery under Miriam's sandals, the wooden hand rail rough and scraping under her hand. She lifted her hand off the rail, afraid of a splinter, and knew she was hesitating, delaying the inevitable.

Her father and husband had forced her into submission. Harsh and brutal words from her father. More words and beatings from her husband had reinforced the message.

Now, she was in the position of possibly doing something similar to this woman.

The realization made her stomach churn, but this Debra, or whatever her name was, potentially held the answer to the people behind Asher's murder and Nurval's death. They needed to know who she really was.

Miriam wiped a hand across her face, felt the dust and grit smear under her touch. She must look hideous, and perhaps that would frighten Debra into talking.

"I'm right here," Jacob said softly behind her. His hand reached out, squeezed the fingers of her right hand. She squeezed back, climbed the last three steps, went through the doorway into the room, leaving it partly open.

The late afternoon sun shone a column of bright orange light through the narrow window high on the right wall as Miriam entered the room. There was a rough wooden table and chair under the window, a pallet and straw mattress against the far wall, and a chipped chamber pot on the left just inside the door. There was a sour smell from the chamber pot that mingled with a musty, unused feel to the room.

The shaft of sunlight left the rest of the room in twilight, and it was a moment before Miriam saw Debra in the chair under the window. There was a plate of food on the table in front of her that looked untouched.

Debra sat with legs curled under her, hands in the lap. She looked up as Miriam came in.

Something sparked in Debra's eyes.

Hope, Miriam thought, and felt a twist in her stomach that she was about to kill that flame.

Something must have shown on her face. Miriam watched the hope disappear from Debra's eyes, replaced with fear and resignation. Her shoulders slumped, and her fingers twisted together.

Without getting too close and seeing the difference in their ages, this woman bore a strong resemblance to the Debra Miriam had met at Ruth's shop.

Miriam kept her voice level and even, just like she had learned to do when she wanted to avoid a beating from her husband.

"What's your real name?"

"Naomi," the woman said, not even trying to pretend. Her head was down now, and her dark hair fell forward over her face, eyes focused on the gaps in the planks of the wood floor.

"Why did you pretend to be Debra?"

"They threatened my mother."

"You told us she died."

A shake of the head, and the dark tresses swung from side to side.

Naomi lifted her head. Even in the shadows, Miriam saw the sheen of tears in the other woman's eyes.

"Some men took her from our home in Borsippa. Two others waited and brought me here."

"To the caravan grounds?"

Naomi nodded, lifted her hand and pointed vaguely at the left wall. "Over there, I think. When you brought me to this place, I was afraid you were with them and were taking me back."

Miriam remembered the fear in Naomi when they had first entered the caravan grounds.

Now she understood why.

"What were you supposed to do?"

"Find out what Asher told you. I'm not sure who he was other than being Judean. They made me learn the story about us being together, so you'd have sympathy. I don't think they expected you to hide me away. I was told to learn what I could and go back to them."

She gestured toward the wall again. "Then they would let us go."

Miriam doubted that.

"You keep pointing toward the wall," Miriam said. "Tell me more about the place."

"It's where the Marduk temple keeps their herds when they come in from the fields. There are buildings where they store feed and birth the lambs. That's where my mother is being held."

Miriam raised her voice. "Jacob, did you hear all this?"

She felt his presence in the doorway, saw Naomi hunch her shoulders, shrink back inside herself.

"I will not hurt you," Jacob said in a calm and even voice, as he came and stood beside Miriam.

She glanced at him, and even though his face was in shadow, she recognized the look on his face. There was some doubt about the story Naomi had told, but also sympathy for her situation.

"Tell us what you can about the buildings," Jacob said in the same even voice.

Some of the fear and tension eased from Naomi's body. She uncurled her legs, sat forward, and her voice was stronger. "I think we are close to the pens. The buildings are on the far side, with a road running alongside. Some rooms are like enclosed barns, others are lots of small rooms for sleeping or storage. I don't know where my mother is."

Miriam glanced at Jacob again. He was nodding in agreement.

"Are the doors secured in any way?" he asked.

"Some are," Naomi said. "Others, especially in the barns, are open and you can just walk in."

Naomi's voice faltered, and then the fear was back in her voice. "What will happen to me?"

Miriam looked at her, remembered the sight of Asher's broken and battered body. "You'll disappear, Naomi," she said.

CHAPTER TWENTY-THREE

The tenth day of Abu - Evening

Jacob adjusted the belt around his waist for what seemed like the hundredth time. The belt wouldn't lie properly and kept twisting, forcing the sword scabbard to knock against his leg as he walked.

Sibri limped slowly along on his right side, and around them in the late twilight turned the barns, stables, and animal pens into dark, unfamiliar shadows.

Away to the right, lanterns flickered, flared, and swayed like fireflies in a frenzy. There were shouts and cries as mules and camels brayed and snorted in protest at something their handlers were doing.

"They should leave whatever it is until daylight, or someone will get hurt," Sibri muttered, then to Jacob. "Are you sure this is a good idea?"

"I haven't had a good idea since I found Asher in my courtyard," Jacob said. To the east there was a flicker of lightning and a growl of thunder as a commentary on his words. He would welcome a storm and rain to ease the heat that seemed more oppressive each day.

Jacob swung his right arm in a circle to ease the stiffness from the bruising, wished Miriam had brought her yarrow salve so he could ease the ache in his arm and shoulder.

Miriam had argued long and hard with him about this expedition and only relented when he agreed to bring Sibri with him. Sibri knew the caravan grounds well enough to guide Jacob in the darkness, and had spent time around the animal pens owned by the temple of Marduk.

"We're going to find Naomi's mother, get her out of there, and then you will take both of them south to my friend Micah in Erech."

"Is it wise to ignore Arioch's travel ban?"

"He banned trading permits," Jacob said. "There's no ban on travel."

"There might be when he hears about this," Sibri grumbled, then tugged at the sleeve of Jacob's robe.

"Take care. There's a fence coming up."

Jacob slowed his pace and made out the two lines of deeper darkness, one at waist height, the other level with his shins. He placed his hands on the upper fence rail and swung his legs over, favoring his left arm as he did so.

The movement brought beads of sweat to Jacob's forehead, slicked his palms, and woke up every bruise in his body. He wiped his palms and forehead on the sleeve of his robe.

"Show man," Sibri said as he ducked under and shuffled through the gap between the rails to join Jacob.

When Sibri was balanced once more on his feet, he looked around him, like he could see everything as clearly as he would in daylight.

He pointed just to the left of straight ahead. "The barns and other buildings are over there. The pens are to our right. There have been no animals here for two moons or more, but tread carefully."

Jacob allowed himself a brief smile as they started across the open ground.

Quite the pair they were, he thought. Sibri with his injured leg and limp. Jacob himself with a sore arm and a body covered with bruises that throbbed and ached with every step.

As they moved, their perspective changed, and they were a dozen paces from the first barn when Jacob saw the yellowish glow of a lantern.

Sibri hissed a warning.

"I see it," Jacob whispered. He moved his hand to the right side of his waist, gripped the hilt of the sword, and loosened it in the leather scabbard. He had taken the sword from the collection used to arm members of the caravans. The weight felt wrong, and awkward in his hands, and he prayed he would have no use for the sword tonight. He also knew if Naomi's mother was guarded, there might be no choice.

They passed into the deeper shadow of the first barn, and the smell of sheep and goat dung hung heavy in the baking air.

"Now you walk carefully," Sibri said, and Jacob was sure Siri laughed as he spoke.

Jacob wasn't sure if the other man was serious or making a joke. To be certain, he placed his feet with care as they crossed the barn.

The heat became more oppressive the further they moved into the barn, the air so still it felt like a physical barrier. On the far side, they came to a closed door that barred the way forward.

Jacob wiped his forehead again, then eased the sword from the scabbard. He held it at an angle to deflect any attack as Sibri pulled the door open a crack.

A shaft of dull yellow light came through the opening. Sibri stopped pulling on the door. There was enough light for Jacob to see the nervousness in Sibri's eyes. He gave the other man's shoulder a reassuring squeeze and angled his head so he could see what was on the other side of the door.

The light came from a torch in a sconce about halfway along the hallway. The torch guttered and flared, giving off a dark smoke that sent the pungent smell of sulfur along the narrow hallway. Too narrow for Jacob and Sibri to walk side-by-side, and barely wide enough to swing a sword.

Jacob leaned close to Sibri, whispered in the other man's ear. "There's no-one there. A bitumen torch is halfway down on the right. I counted four doorways on the left, and a door at the far end. I'll lead."

Sibri gave a soft grunt of assent, pulled the door wider so Jacob could go through.

The bitumen smell was stronger inside, some from the torch, some from the black lines of bitumen that sealed the gaps between the planks of wood. The sulfur stink was almost enough to make Jacob's eyes water.

Jacob kept the sword angled down from left to right across his body. There was no room for a sideways swing in the narrow hallway. He would have to slash in a down to up strike if they met anyone.

The first two rooms were empty, with pieces of straw scattered across the floor. Store rooms, Jacob guessed. A guess confirmed by the bales of straw stacked in the third room.

The fourth room had a door and a palm log across the door to keep it closed.

Jacob walked past the door, stopped, and gestured to Sibri that he should open the door.

The caravan master nodded, sheathed his own sword. Sibri struggled with the log until he shifted his body and leaned the log against the wall.

"Jacob," Sibri hissed as he pulled the door open.

Jacob backed up three paces, glanced away from the hallway, and into the room.

The bitumen torch gave little light into the room, but Jacob could make out the shape of a person sat on the side of a pallet.

The head came up, and Jacob had the feeling of being assessed.

"Can you walk?" Jacob asked.

"I walked in here, young man. I'm sure I can walk out." A firm voice, cracking a little with age.

Jacob knew she couldn't see his smile in the low light. He heard the determination in her voice, sensed she wouldn't be a burden to Sibri.

"My partner here, Sibri, is going to take you out of here, to Naomi. In the morning, he will take you both to a friend of mine in Erech."

"And if I choose not to go to Erech?"

"That is your choice, but I won't be able to protect you, and whatever I achieve tonight, I doubt those who imprisoned you will let you live the next time."

The woman gave a long sigh. Jacob saw the dark shape of her twist and turn off the pallet until she was standing, the straw crackling as she moved. Her first steps were hesitant. She paused, rolled her neck and back. Her next steps were easier, more confident.

She reached the doorway, screwed her eyes closed, blinked, looked at Jacob and Sibri, back to Jacob, and said. "Where will you be?"

"Seeing who else is here," Jacob said.

He gave the woman a gentle nudge toward Sibri, made sure the two were headed back toward the barn, then turned to the door at the far end of the hallway.

The door opened into another hallway, twice as long as the previous hallway, and wider this time. Still not quite wide enough to fully swing a sword from side-to-side. There were two bitumen torches spaced along the right wall, which here was mud brick.

Jacob ducked his head into the first room he came to. There was a table in the middle of the room, a long narrow window high on the opposite wall, and below it a waxed board like the one he'd seen in Arioch's office. There wasn't enough light to see any writing on the board. He doubted the boards meant anything for his search.

The next room was the same. As Jacob stepped back into the hallway, he heard the murmur of voices. He moved to the right side of the hallway to give his sword arm as much space as possible.

Jacob rested there for a moment, the ache in his right arm burning, the bruises on his midsection itching from where his robe scraped the skin. The sensible approach, he knew, was to follow Sibri and Naomi's mother, send a message to Ligish and bring the temple guard here in the morning.

Except there was no guarantee they'd find anything in the morning.

And the tone and cadence of one speaker sounded familiar.

The conversation came from the fifth room, the one closest to the far door.

Jacob guessed there were two or three men talking. He eased up onto the balls of his feet and pushed forward slowly as a fresh voice said.

"Why did you allow the woman to escape?"

That voice Jacob recognized too well. The anger and fury at the betrayal washed over him.

Ligish!

Jacob lifted the sword, ready to charge into the room. The fury boiled up inside him, warring with the intense disappointment. He trusted this man. Asher had trusted him.

His first target would be Ligish. Deal with that traitor, and argue with Arioch after.

Jacob took a step forward, paused, forced himself to relax.

How many times had he counseled his soldiers to think calmly before acting?

More than he could count, Jacob reminded himself. There would be a reckoning with Ligish, and soon.

He took a long breath, reassessed what he knew, or thought he knew.

Including Ligish, Jacob now guessed there were four men in the room.

Possibly more.

A headlong rush into the room was likely to get him killed and achieve nothing.

"It was a failure by the men sent for the Judean. We lost nothing from it," the familiar voice again, rough and harsh, interrupted Jacob's thoughts.

He still couldn't recall when or where he'd heard that voice.

Distracted, Jacob missed the next words, realized someone was leaving the room almost too late.

Quickly, Jacob retreated into the nearest room. He pressed himself against the wall inside the door as a man hurried past, going the way Jacob had come from.

Jacob waited until he heard rushing footsteps as the man returned. Jacob judged his moment, stepped out into the hallway, sword extended, angled to strike up and under the ribs. The man, intent on his own problems - the missing woman - impaled himself on the blade almost before he realized Jacob was there.

The man opened his mouth to cry out, but Jacob was on him. He pushed the sword deeper, leaned over and clamped a hand over the man's mouth so no sound escaped.

Jacob dragged the body into the darkened room where he'd hidden. He checked the dead man for a weapon, found nothing, and extracted the sword he'd used. He wiped the blade clean on the dead man's robe.

The weight of the weapon still felt awkward, unfamiliar, and uncomfortable.

Not for the first time that evening, Jacob cursed himself for not bringing his own sword.

Jacob stood in the partial darkness, the odor of spilled blood heavy on the hot air, trying to decide his best course of action. Judging from the body on the floor, it was likely none of the men in the room were armed, except Ligish.

Ligish would have a sword, and likely a knife or two. And he was good, probably better than Jacob at the moment after the beating Jacob had taken two nights ago.

The option to leave remained. Jacob took a half pace in that direction when he realized the most likely person tasked with the follow up was Ligish. It was a certainty in Jacob's mind that Ligish the traitor would find no trace of any wrongdoing.

The option to leave really didn't exist.

Jacob hefted the sword in his left hand to get a better feel for the balance, walked out into the hallway and was face to face with a man who came through the far door.

The man shook off his surprise, cried out in alarm as Jacob rushed forward. There was no space to use the sword effectively. Jacob used the force behind his rush to pin the man in the corner between the door and the wall.

The man's breath was sour on Jacob's face, his dark eyes in the light of the bitumen torches, awash with fear. Jacob heard a commotion in the room, now behind him. No sense any longer in being quiet or hiding.

Jacob lifted his knee into the other man's groin, slammed his head against the wall. Then a second time, left a smear of blood on the rough wood.

Jacob let the man fall, cursed at the way the uneven balance of the sword dragged at his arm, and went into the room.

Four bitumen torches and a pair of sesame oil lamps made the room as bright as day.

There were three people in the room. A room easily three times the size of the others Jacob had been in. Subisha slumped down on a couch, looking barely conscious. There was a man hanging from a hook in the ceiling. He was naked, his body flecked with cuts and blood.

Ligish!

Not a traitor.

The wash of relief interrupted Jacob's concentration and was and nearly his undoing.

The third man, Makru, and now Jacob knew why the voice was familiar, came at him with a short sword, swinging wildly. Jacob blocked and parried. Silver, gold and orange sparks erupted as the blades came together with crashes and clangs that echoed around the room.

Another thrust and parry, and Jacob found himself close to Makru. They were much the same height, eyes level with each other.

"I'll enjoy killing you, Judean. I'll leave your body in the dust where I left your countryman."

Makru's left fist lifted then. He punched Jacob three times high on the right arm. Short, vicious jabs that landed on the old wound and the bruises from two nights before.

The pain seared. Ripped up through Jacob's arm, across his chest and into his head. The room went gray.

Jacob stumbled back. His hip hit a table, tipping him off balance, and he barely lifted the sword to ward off a swinging strike. As he went over backwards, Jacob lashed out with his foot, felt the crunch as he connected with the inside of Makru's right knee.

Makru hopped back as Jacob hit the floor.

On the far side of the room, Subisha shook his head, ran his hand over his face.

Jacob rolled, coming up into a crouch beside Ligish, who said. "Kill him for me."

Jacob didn't have the breath for a reply. Barely the breath to push to his feet. His right arm had no feeling, hung useless by his side.

This had to end quickly, or Makru would win.

The wooden table made an excellent support. As Jacob stood, he saw the knives on the table, four of them, all stained and slick with fresh blood. The knives had no handle, just a small ball on the end that turned into a slender, narrow, wicked looking blade.

He dropped the sword on the table, snatched the first knife, flung it at Makru, making the priest duck. Jacob tossed another knife, and in the scant time he made for himself, took more care with the third.

He grabbed the sword, nearly dropped it, fumbled it in his fingers, and followed the trajectory of the knife, felt a surge of satisfaction as the knife buried deep into Makru's shoulder.

And then he was on top of the man, left shoulder down and driving Makru back. They tumbled over another table, Makru underneath, and he screamed high and loud as they crashed to the floor and the knife in his shoulder twisted and drove deeper.

Jacob was on his feet first, the sword finally firm in his grip. He pressed the point against Makru's throat.

"Kill him!"

"No!"

Subisha struggled to his feet, tottered unsteadily, then sat heavily down on the couch.

"No," he said again. "Makru must answer to the temple."

Jacob gave Ligish an apologetic look, reversed the sword in his grip, and slammed the hilt onto Makru's forehead.

CHAPTER TWENTY-FOUR

The thirteenth day of Abu - Evening

In the past three days, a line of thunderstorms had rolled over Babylon, and dissipated the intense heat. The weather was still warm, but for now; the sun didn't have the intensity to burn exposed skin.

Jacob was grateful for the change, even if it only lasted for a few days. He reclined on a couch in Isaac's courtyard, the stairs to the upper levels on his left, the doorway to the street on his right. He could just make out the shape of Solly as he sat in his cool niche, watching the street and the courtyard at the same time.

Jacob heard the chatter of the servants in the kitchen as they prepared the evening meal, caught the smell of roasting goat mingled with garlic, and felt his mouth water at the prospect of the meal.

Around the courtyard, from one end to the other, Isaac's boys played a chase game with shrill shouts and cries as they scampered between and around the couches and tables.

Jacob wondered how it would feel in a few years if these were his sons, and decided he liked the idea.

One boy misjudged a step. His hip hit a chair, and he stumbled against the table. Jacob moved swiftly to catch a pair of goblets, as they tilted perilously. He caught them before the wine spilled.

The sudden movement jarred Jacob's right arm. He winced as a flare of pain lanced along his right side and up into his neck, making him dizzy.

Miriam had wrapped a length of linen round his right wrist and looped it over his head to support his arm and prevent him from moving it too much. He had grumbled, and complained, but had to admit his arm felt much better with the support.

"Let me. You're supposed to be resting," Miriam said, appearing from behind him, taking the goblets away in a single smooth sweep of her hands.

"I am resting," he said, grateful for the help, and eased back onto the couch. He smiled at her attempt to be stern and scolding. "I have no option. There's no one for me to talk with."

It was Miriam's turn to smile as she tucked her robe under her legs and sat beside him.

"I told Isaac and Esther to leave you alone. There'll be plenty of time for talking when we eat," she said. Then. "You know you could have lost that arm?"

Jacob nodded, reached for the goblet Miriam had saved, and took a drink of the Nineveh wine.

"It's something I fear every time it gets knocked, even on innocent occasions."

Losing his right arm had been the one thing he feared when he felt the numbness immediately after subduing Makru.

He had feeling again, but the arm had been numb for nearly a full day, and he could tell from the tight expression on Miriam's face she was still worried.

The last time his arm was numb like this was during the journey into Exile. On that occasion, it had been nearly three days before the feeling returned.

Jacob decided not to mention that to Miriam.

When he focused back on Miriam, Jacob saw she had something tucked under her arm and a strange expression on her face.

"Is something wrong?" he asked.

Miriam shook her head, looked at him full on. Jacob saw the strange look on her face was uncertainty.

"I know this is against tradition, but you gave your shawl to Asher. This is for you," she said, and offered him a bulky bundle wrapped in fine white cloth.

Jacob placed his wine goblet on the table as she handed him the bundle.

"We are very close to being married," he said, having guessed what was wrapped inside the cloth.

Using the fingers of his left hand, Jacob teased open the folds of cloth and ran his fingers through the soft wool of the new prayer shawl. He saw the knots on the fringe, the way they were tied, the way they lay flat.

"You tied these knots?" he said, his voice choking a little as he said the words.

Miriam nodded.

Jacob dipped his head, took a long swallow to clear the lump in his throat. He was only partly successful and vowed he would make Miriam's herb room a very special place.

"This is perhaps the most wonderful gift I have ever received," he said, untangled his right arm from the sling, reached over and took her hand.

She moved closer until he didn't have to stretch and they sat in a companionable silence until there was the sound of someone arriving at the street door.

They were too far away to hear the words, but Solly's tone was welcoming. When Jacob looked up, Ligish stood just inside the courtyard, almost at a military attention. He wore tan trews and a sand-colored loose-fitting tunic with long sleeves that came down over his hands, almost hiding the rope burns on his wrists. Ligish saw Jacob, lifted a hand in acknowledgment, and walked forward with care and precision like every movement caused him pain.

Jacob watched and remembered the naked body he saw two nights before, with dozens of cuts and slashes. Each wound in a muscle or tender area that would take time to heal and stop hurting.

"Will you get us another jug of the Nineveh wine?" Jacob said to Miriam in a low voice as he stood to greet Ligish.

"I missed you at the Esagila earlier," Ligish said as he reached Jacob, and the two men clasped wrists.

"I wanted to look for you, but Arioch was insistent I be escorted directly to the gates with no detours." Jacob said, helping Ligish to a seat. "Miriam will be here with wine in a moment, then we can talk."

Ligish eased himself down and back onto the cushions. When he was settled, he breathed a long sigh of relief.

"The wine will be most welcome," he said. "And for the best, you followed instructions this time. The Esagila is in turmoil with every piece of information Makru gives us."

"He's co-operating?" Jacob asked.

"Not willingly."

Jacob suppressed a shudder. He had never seen the cells beneath the Esagila, and never wanted to. He suspected the wounds on Ligish's body were nothing compared to how Makru now looked. Jacob thought about Asher and Debra's husband, and felt no sympathy.

Miriam arrived with the jug of the Nineveh wine. Jacob's sour mood began to fade. She exchanged a few words with Ligish, then left the two men alone.

The look of appreciation on Ligish's face after his first mouthful finished the job.

"I see why Arioch was so upset about you buying up the harvest for the next two years," Ligish said.

"Let's hope the future harvests are the same quality, or better," Jacob said. "Arioch will be equally upset if all we deliver to him is expensive vinegar."

Jacob thought back to the bartering in Arioch's rooms. They had argued back and forth, giving and taking, proposing and suggesting, until an agreement was reached.

Most importantly for Jacob, Arioch had removed the ban on travel, and for that, Jacob would have traded away every jug of the Nineveh wine.

"How is Subisha?" Jacob asked, refilling their goblets.

"He leaves for Haran tomorrow," Ligish said. "He is the priest escorting Nurval's body, and will remain in Haran to consult with priests at the temple of the moon."

"Do you know who replaces Subisha?" Jacob asked.

He let his mind walk through the list of priests in the Esagila who might be considered, balanced what he knew of their abilities against their attitude to Judeans.

It took Jacob a moment to place the name Ligish gave him. Dajjan. And then he remembered. Dajjan was the priest who attended the wedding of Horam and Damkina. A priest, Arioch, told him to pay attention to.

"Arioch doesn't need to be chief priest, does he?"

Ligish smiled as he took another sip of wine. "Arioch has achieved what Makru tried to do. He will be the power of the Esagila for many years to come, and without the problems of being chief priest. What of your people? Debra, and the other one?"

"Debra is staying with Rachel and Samuel. The other one, Naomi. She and her mother must be halfway to Erech by now. My friend Micah will see them settled safely."

Ligish nodded, then said. "You understand one day in the future, this Micah will send you some of his discards and rejects and it will cause you a lot of trouble."

His face became serious. He placed the wine goblet on the table, turned slowly and stiffly so he was facing Jacob.

"Two nights ago," Ligish said. "You were ready to kill me. I saw it on your face when you came into the room where Makru was holding me."

"I was in the hallway." Jacob said. "I only heard your voice, and the words. Until I came into the room, I thought you were working with Makru. It's rare that I'm pleased to be wrong about something. This is one of those times. What were you doing there?"

"If I were a traitor, you should have killed me," Ligish said with a grim smile.

"Why was I there?" Another smile, equally grim. "Arrogance and hubris like you, I think. I knew Nurval wasn't negotiating with Arioch, so it seemed reasonable he was dealing with Subisha, or should I say, Makru."

Ligish took a sip of wine. "I was careless and would prefer not to talk of it any more."

Then his face lightened. "Instead, I am here drinking your wine, and I also have news. One of the army messengers passed your Judah caravan. The messenger estimated they are maybe a moon's travel from Babylon, maybe a little further. You should expect them any time from the middle of Elulu, and certainly before the month of Tehritsu."

Before Tehritsu.

Jacob glanced across the courtyard to where Miriam stood outside the kitchen. She and Esther were deep in discussion about something, probably the upcoming meal.

Miriam's ebony hair shone in the light of the westering sun, and her face glowed like it was a sun of its own. Jacob felt a shift of something deep inside him, the way it always did when he watched Miriam.

"The smile on your face tells me that is excellent news," Ligish said.

"Very excellent news," Jacob agreed. "It means Miriam and I can marry before Rosh Hashanah, our new year. We expect you to be there as well."

"It will be an honor to attend," Ligish said, and Jacob saw the pleasure on his face was genuine.

And Asher would be there, Jacob knew.

Not in body, but in their hearts.

There's a line in the climax of Death at a Wedding, the book before this one, where Jacob has a flashback to his unit of soldiers during the siege of Jerusalem. It was that line that triggered the idea for this book. It was the first time those characters became real to me, and I had a glimpse of their story.

I have a title and notes for the first two chapters of the story of those men during the siege of Jerusalem. For now, that's all there is, but I know the rest will reveal itself once I focus on those first two chapters.

One of the fun things about writing historical fiction is the research and background reading that happens before, during, and sometimes after the writing.

For Asher's burial preparations, I leaned heavily on Hayyim Schauss's book The Lifetime of a Jew, and a 2004 article from Religion and Ethics Newsweekly titled Jewish Burial Practices.

Tradition has it that men prepare men for burial, and women prepare women. When Jacob asks Miriam to prepare Asher's body, he admits the break from tradition. I have nothing to support the supposition. I suspect over the years, similar situations arose, and accommodations were made and ask forgiveness if I've crossed any lines.

As usual *Daily Life in Ancient Mesopotamia* by Karen Rhea Nemet-Nejat was invaluable in making sure I got simple things like food and clothing correct.

Once again, a huge thank you to Jackie and Kim for reading the manuscript and pointing out spelling, grammar and consistency errors. Any that remain are my fault.

ABOUT THE AUTHOR

International selling author Richard Freeborn writes in many genres from historical and mystery to romance and thrillers.

Currently Richard writes stories in several series including historical mysteries set in Ancient Babylon, the Dune Crest current day mysteries, the time travel Puzzle Store series, and contemporary romances set in Diamond Beach, somewhere along Florida's panhandle.

For more information about Richard's books and projects, please visit his website at www.richardfreeborn.com

You can find Richard's books here: books2read.com/RichardFreeborn/

COMING SOON

THE MURDER OF A DEAD MAN

CHAPTER ONE

The Eighteenth day Elulu - Late Afternoon

The late afternoon sun dipped behind the tallest buildings of Babylon's temple complex, the Esagila. Jacob felt the heat of the day fade away as the shadows grew and the light lost the harsh glare of the day.

Jacob wiped the sweat from his brow, leaned against the mud-brick wall that was the outside wall of the extensive kitchen he had built for the house.

A house where he would bring his new bride, Miriam, once they were married in less than a month.

Jacob had met Miriam by chance, some two years after the people of Judah were Exiled to Babylon after the fall and sack of Jerusalem. They kept meeting through her cousin's husband Isaac, and his brother Amos.

It had taken another six months for the dislike between them to become respect, then friendship, and much to Jacob's surprise, love.

His marriage in Jerusalem had been arranged, as had Miriam's.

Jacob's wife had died in child birth with their son. Miriam's husband, a priest, had disappeared during the trek into Exile.

Jacob shook his head at the thoughts and memories, and marveled at how Yahweh, found a way to bring them together.

A story to tell our children, Jacob thought, then laughed aloud. The noise bounced around the courtyard and made it seem like there were many other people with him.

He and Miriam were at least ten years older than most married couples who started a family, both here in Babylon or at home in Jerusalem. It was unlikely they'd be blessed with sons and daughters. Jacob had built the house with that hope, and if the children never arrived, there were plenty of rooms for guests and visitors.

Jacob let his gaze run around the courtyard again, taking in the mud-brick walls, and the beams of Lebanese cedar supporting the roof. He felt his chest swell with pride at the work, most of which he had done himself.

It was a good house, and it would be a good home for them, whether children came or not.

Jacob checked the angle of the sun once more. He had promised to eat the evening meal at Isaac's house and if he didn't leave now, the Marduk Gate into the city would be closed with no entry until the next morning.

He pushed off the wall, his mind already on the conversation with Isaac. Several months ago they had sent a caravan to trade with the Judeans left in Jerusalem. The caravan was expected back in Babylon soon, and Jacob wanted to discuss with Isaac where they might find buyers for the goods on the caravan. It was expected that most of the goods, especially the valuable items, would be offered first to the priests at the temple of Marduk.

Jacob had a good relationship with several of the priests at the temple of Marduk. Better than the relationship with most of his own priests.

The thought brought another smile on his face as he reached the edge of the courtyard. He started onto the track that led east alongside the orchard of almond trees and down to the road for the Marduk Gate.

Ahead of him a pair of birds took flight from the trees, chirping and squawking as they whirled and wheeled above the branches.

Jacob heard it then.

The soft clip-clop of a horse moving slowly along the stone path.

Jacob stepped back into the shadow of the trees, careful to walk without making any noise. His left hand reached for a sword, then stopped as he remembered he had left the sword at his house inside the city walls.

He wasn't really worried, but he wasn't expecting any visitors either, and sometimes it was better to be cautious, or just stay with old habits that were hard to discard.

Jacob bent down, scooped a pair of rounded flat stones from the ground beside the twisted roots of an almond tree. They weren't much of a weapon but they would suffice.

Jacob stayed in the shadows. He let the scent of the almond blossom wrap around him as he listened to the birds and the sound of the horse.

A moment later, he saw the horse, and the rider.

It took Jacob a long moment to recognize the man on the horse as the animal picked it's way slowly along the track beside the almond orchard.

The man was thinner, healthier, and had a light in his gray eyes that Jacob had never seen before. He scanned the track and the orchard, his eyes sliding past Jacob twice.

Jacob let the stones slip from his hand, barely heard the thud as they hit the ground, and stepped forward into the open.

The movement made the horse shy away. The rider brought it back under control with a quick tug of the reins, and a soft word of encouragement.

"Amos?" Jacob said, although he couldn't keep the question from his tone.

This time the man started. He frowned. A frown that became an easy smile when he recognized Jacob.

"As ever was," Amos said.

He eased the horse to a halt, dismounted in an easy swing of his leg. Amos stood there for a moment, then kneaded his fists into the small of his back as he looked around the courtyard and the house.

"You built all this yourself?"

"Mostly," Jacob said, feeling the surge of pride ripple through again him as he admitted to the work. This one felt better though, because it was someone whose opinion he trusted.

"I had some help with the well in the kitchen and the plumbing."

Jacob watched as Amos gave a nod. He walked over to the kitchen wall, ran his hand along the line of bricks, gave another nod.

"This is good work."

Jacob smiled his thanks, then said. "I heard from the people at the temple of Marduk, the caravan was close. I didn't expect to see anyone for another day or two."

"Some of us came on ahead," Amos said.

There was something in his tone. Something about the way his face changed from approval and admiration of the building work to something else that sent a frisson of fear through Jacob's body.

"What happened, Amos? Is everyone safe?"

If the trade goods were gone, it would be hard; crippling probably, but that meant nothing if people were lost. People he knew and cared for.

Jacob offered up a quick prayer there were no deaths.

Amos sighed. "Everyone is safe. It's not what you think."

Jacob wasn't so sure.

He kept silent, waited for Amos to continue.

"It happened on the return. We were about a day's travel south of Rabat Amman when we found a man wandering in the desert. He's a Judean."

Jacob frowned. He was relieved about the caravan but something nagged at him about the story Amos told.

"Tell me everything," he said, leading Amos all the way into the courtyard and sitting him on one of the newly made couches.

Amos pushed his hand back through his hair. "The man we found and brought with us to Babylon is a Judean and a priest."

His head dropped and he turned away, but not before Jacob saw the sheen of tears in Amos's gray eyes.

Amos sobbed once, his back heaved as he took a long breath.

He kept his head down.

"I'm so sorry, Jacob. The priest's name is Nahum. He's Miriam's husband."

ALSO BY RICHARD FREEBORN

Thieves in the Temple

Jacob fought desperately to save Jerusalem from the Babylonian invaders. Injured and exiled, Jacob builds a new life among his former enemies in the city of Babylon.

As the Babylonians celebrate their New Year, Jacob uncovers a conspiracy threatening the freedom and lives of every Exile.

Uncertain who to trust Jacob unravels the threads of deceit into a compelling climax that saves not just the Exiles, but Jacob himself.

Get Thieves in the Temple, the first Jacob and Miriam mystery at: books2read. com/Thieves

Death at a Wedding

Jacob fought desperately to save Jerusalem from the Babylonian invaders. Injured and exiled, Jacob now builds a new life among his former enemies in the city of Babylon.

An unexpected death makes Jacob reassess everything he believes. Are his friends being truthful. Are the priests honest, or are darker forces at work in Babylon?

Pulling back the layers of lies and half-truths leads Jacob to a shocking last confrontation.

Get Death at a Wedding, the second Jacob and Miriam mystery at: https://books2read.com/DeathataWedding

The Corpse in the Courtyard

Jacob is devastated when he discovers the body of an old friend dumped at his home. The murder drags him into a conspiracy he's tried to avoid for many months. At odds with his own people, and the priests of the Babylonian temple, Jacob must rely on Miriam to determine truths and falsehoods from people neither of them trust.

It takes another violent death to point Jacob and Miriam in the right direction. A direction that threatens to cost Jacob his life, and condemn every Judean Exile into slavery.

Get The Corpse in the Courtyard, the third Jacob and Miriam mystery at:
https://books2read.com/TheCorpseInTheCourtyard

Babylon Collections

Beginnings in Babylon
books2read.com/BeginningsInBabylon

Unexpected Companions
books2read.com/u/38yXv7

Making a New Start
books2read.com/NewStart

The Puzzle Store

Tales from the Puzzle Store

books2read.com/Puzzle

Christmas at the Puzzle Store

books2read.com/u/bxa7oe

Other Collections

Call Me Rhys

books2read.com/CallMeRhys

The Vatican Shadows

books2read.com/VaticanShadows

Mageweaver

books2read.com/Mageweaver

A Frailty of Heroes

books2read.com/Frailty

A Bag of Bodies

books2read.com/BagOfBodies

The Beach Bar on the Dune

https://books2read.com/u/3GJlod

From Ceres to Vesta

https://books2read.com/u/brEaeM

Where Infinity Begins

https://books2read.com/u/47091N

www.ingramcontent.com/pod-product-compliance
Lightning Source LLC
Chambersburg PA
CBHW070505200726
48293CB00007B/2389